Death
OR
ICE CREAM?

~ OR ~ ICE CREAM?

Gareth P. Jones

David R. Godine, *Publisher* · Boston

For
Natalie Foster and Findbar Good
(who both chose ice cream)

Published in 2017 by
David R. Godine, *Publisher*
Post Office Box 450
Jaffrey, New Hampshire 03452
www.godine.com

Copyright © 2016 by Gareth P. Jones.
Illustrations copyright © 2016 Adam Stower.

First Published in Great Britain by Hot Key Books in 2016.

A CIP catalogue record for this book is available from the
Library of Congress
ISBN 978-1-56792-610-1
LCCN 2017034665

Second printing, 2017
Printed in the United States

Death or Ice Cream?

"Death or ice cream? Which one, my friend?"
I said to the waiter, "Which do you recommend?"
The waiter replied, "Now, I'm sure I can't say
But I'll give you my thoughts about that anyway."
"Ice cream's refreshing and melts on your tongue.
It's sweeter than death but it won't last as long.
Ice cream is perfect for ending a meal
But if you want endings, death's the real deal.
The thing is with ice cream, you don't have to eat it
But you can't deny death. You can fight but not beat it,
You cannot refuse it, avoid, hide or lose it.
Death selects you. You don't have to choose it."
I looked at the waiter and then understood
When I noticed the scythe, the cloak and the hood.
"Your time is up," said his calming voice,
And I knew death or ice cream wasn't a choice.

The Anecdote

1.

ALBERT DANCE had a lifelong dislike of door-to-door salespeople. Knocking on someone's private door in order to flog cleaning fluids, kitchen knives or life insurance felt like an awful intrusion. He was about to slam the door in the impudent fellow's face when he noticed the vial of deep purple liquid in his hand.

"What is it?" demanded Albert.

The grey-suited man looked at Albert over the top of his spectacles. "Hello. Yes. I'm in the area selling anecdotes."

"I'm sorry, I'm rather busy," replied Albert.

"I can see that. Celebrating are we?" The man indicated the large glass of whiskey in Albert's hand.

"This isn't for me. I was taking it to my mother upstairs. She is not well. Not well at all."

"I'm sorry to hear that. Bedridden, is she? The ill, they put such a strain on the well, don't they? How long has it been this way?"

"I forget how long."

"What a doting son you must be."

Albert heard his mother banging on the floor, as she often did. "That's her now," he said. "I must take her medicine up."

"This really won't take long."

"What is it an antidote to?" asked Albert, looking at the purple vial.

The salesman adjusted his glasses self-consciously, rather like a bad stage actor who had just remembered what he was supposed to do at this point in the play. "I'm afraid you misunderstand me," he said. "I don't sell antidotes. I offer anecdotes, stories . . . memories."

"So what's in the vial?"

"Oh, this is poison," said the man casually.

"Poison?"

"Yes. The essence of death, to give it its full and rather ostentatious name. I am not selling the poison. There's not as much call for it as you might imagine. I am selling an anecdote."

"I don't need any anecdotes. Thank you," said Albert.

He tried to close the door but the salesman stopped it with his foot. "Most of our customers struggle for things to talk about at parties and other social occasions."

"Well, I don't."

"That's wonderful to hear. Perhaps you could enthrall me with one of your witty remembrances. You see, I buy as well as sell."

"Very well. If it will make you go away." Albert told the salesman the story about the time he had found himself at a

4

cardboard conference, having mixed up the dates in his diary. As a specialist dealer in paper with no interest in cardboard, it was a most amusing situation. Albert had told the story several times with varied results but the salesman's intense gaze unnerved him and he stumbled over the punch line, which involved a fellow salesperson offering Albert his card. The salesman listened patiently but blank-faced until he had finished.

"What do you think?" asked Albert. "Are you interested?"

"Not in the least."

"I mean in buying my anecdote."

"I understand. Not in the least. Albert, you don't mind if I call you Albert, do you, Albert? The fact is, Albert, that I have never met a man in more need of an anecdote," he said. "This conference story of yours has some required elements of irony but lacks dramatic tension. I am offering you an anecdote to capture the imaginations of even the most bored dinner party guest."

Albert wondered if the salesman knew about his last dinner party where all three of his guests had ended up face down in the baked Alaska, fast asleep.

"How much do they cost, these anecdotes you're selling?" he asked.

"The only cost is your full, undivided attention."

"Perhaps you should come in."

He led the salesman into the room at the front of his house, which his mother always referred to as the Room for Best.

He heard banging on the floor and looked down at the glass of whiskey. "I should take my mother's medicine up," he said.

"It is unwise to leave strangers in one's house unsupervised," said the salesman. "Especially those bearing poison."

5

"Yes. Of course." Albert placed the whiskey down on the sideboard. "Would you care for a glass of water?"

"I never drink water," replied the salesman.

"Don't you get rather dehydrated?"

"Not at all. Dehydration is a myth created by those who would sell you bottled water and moisturizer. I take all my liquids from dock leaves." The salesman opened his case and pulled out one neatly ironed dock leaf. He carefully rolled it up and lifted it to his mouth and sucked at the end like a cigar. 'Very refreshing," he said, "plus it has tremendous health benefits."

"Is that so?" asked Albert.

"Absolutely. Stinging nettles have no effect on me at all."

"Fascinating. Is this part of the anecdote?"

The salesman's laughter was so sudden and explosive that Albert feared he was in pain. "No," said the salesman. "This is not part of the anecdote. This is chit-chat. Are you ready for the anecdote?"

"I'm not sure. What's it about?"

"It's about you, of course, which is why it will be delivered in the second person."

"The second person?"

"You, Albert. A sickly child—"

"What?"

"This is how the story begins. Now, if you're sitting comfortably, I shall begin."

2.

A sickly child. This was how your mother described you. You were not allowed to play with the other children. Instead you were forced to watch their games from the warm side of the window pane.

You don't remember ever seeing a doctor but one day your mother packed your bags and sent you to Larkin Mills Central Hospital. She drove you there herself. It was the only time she allowed you in the car. She did love that upholstery. When you arrived at the hospital entrance she said, "I would come with you, my darling dear, but parking prices are astronomical these days. It's one of the things we're campaigning against."

Your mother loved her campaigns. You remember the time she chained herself to the town hall to prevent them building a new orphanage in your street. They were happy times.

"You had better go before I get moved on," she said, leaning over you and opening your door.

"What should I do when I get there? We don't know what's wrong with me."

"Tell them that you are ill but have no symptoms. Explain that you are booked into Doctor Good's Wing for Specially Ill Children."

"Will you visit me?" Any tears that rolled down your face went unnoticed by your mother.

"I'll try, my darling dear, but I am terribly busy at the moment. There are all my campaigns and it'll be Garden Open Day before I know it, and you know how all consuming that can be."

"But we haven't got a garden," you protested weakly.

"No, but I'm making the lemonade and everyone raves about my secret recipe."

Your mother's secret recipe was one freshly squeezed lemon, one bottle of cheap gin and two bottles of expensive lemonade.

You watched her drive away, wondering when you would

next see her, then you went into the hospital. The lady sitting at reception ignored you for as long as possible but, when you did not go away, she looked up at you and said, "Yes?"

"I'm here for Doctor Good," you replied.

She eyed the overnight bag your mother had packed for you. "You'll have to leave that here. You can't bring contaminated objects into the hospital."

"It's just my clothes and some books."

"Books? Books are the worst," cried the receptionist. "All those germ-covered hands poring over filthy, porous pages. Goodness, no. We haven't allowed books of any kind into the hospital since the Romance Flu of '89. A terrible business. Someone brought in a stack of cheap romantic titles on the Monday. By the following Friday we were wheeling out so many corpses that Mr. Milkwell had to hire a coach."

The receptionist pulled on a pair of rubber gloves before picking up your bag and dropping it into an unseen drawer. She handed you a paper dressing gown and told you to put it on. You changed in the disabled toilet and placed your clothes in one of the industrial rubbish bags provided.

That day involved a lot of waiting, by the end of which you were lying in the bed near the door of a large room full of other children wired up to beeping machines. They were as still as waxwork models. The nurses only spoke to each other, and rarely about anything to do with the hospital. The children didn't speak at all. You were relieved when a man with silvery grey hair and white coat came to stand beside your bed.

"Hello, Albert. I'm Doctor Good. Can you please tell me what the matter is?" He lifted a clipboard from the end of your bed.

"I'm sickly," you said. "But I don't have any symptoms."

"Yes," he said, shaking his head. "Except everyone has symptoms. I myself suffer from weakness of the knees, aching kidneys and a lacerated happenstance, and yet I'm in perfectly good health."

"Can you make me better?"

"Better at what?" he replied. "Better at tennis? Better behaved? A better person? No. These are improvements you must make yourself." He scribbled frantically on the pad.

"Can't anything be done? I just want to be well and return home."

"There have been studies," he admitted, "but then there are always studies, aren't there? What use are studies to you?"

You admitted you didn't know.

"No. Well, don't worry. You're in good hands. The best, if my awards are anything to go by, but let's not dwell on those."

He flipped the clipboard around to show that he had drawn a sad face. "Do you know what this is?" he asked.

"Is it me?" you replied.

"It's what is known as the human condition," he said. "And you have an acute case of it."

"Is it treatable?"

"Everything is treatable. Well, almost everything. Ingrowing toenails are still very much the exception but even in that area modern medicine is making great progress."

"Do I have those as well?" you asked.

Doctor Good lifted the bed sheet and inspected your toes. "No. All perfectly fine down here. If anything, you have an ingrowing personality, most likely due to lack of sunlight, but all these things will be fixed once we've got you set up. Nurse Grimling, wire him up, please. You may feel some discomfort at first but it's all for the best, I assure you."

An unsmiling nurse appeared and inserted tubes into various points of your body. Some were uncomfortable. Others painful.

"This machine will ensure that all the correct nutrients are fed into your body and that all the bad humors are drawn out," explained Doctor Good. "I'll come back and check on you soon to see whether we can't turn your frown upside down."

He turned his picture the other way up but it didn't look like someone smiling. It looked like an upside-down sad face.

3.

You have no idea how long you were in that hospital. There was no clock in the room and, with the windows painted white, day and night lost their meaning. A tube up your nose fed brown liquid into your stomach so there were no meals to break up the days. Other tubes in other parts of your body extracted fluids. There was no need to move and soon you lost the desire. Sometimes you heard children playing. They sounded near but you could never pick out individual voices. Your mother never came to visit. No one came. You were alone in your pain. Doctor Good sometimes appeared. He would tut and doodle, but he didn't speak to you again and you were no longer strong enough to speak to him.

Your dreams were muddy and confused. Most involved tubes and symphonies of beeping machines. You preferred these dreams to the happy ones. There was nothing worse than running freely down a hill only to wake up and find yourself trapped in the hospital bed. Sometimes you would think about getting up but there was no energy in your limbs.

Then, one day, long after you had given up all hope, you

heard a voice. It wasn't a gossiping nurse but a girl whispering in your ear. "Wake up. Wake up. I need your help."

You opened your eyes and saw her standing by your bed. She was younger than you. She wore a paper dressing gown.

"What's your name?" she asked.

It took you a moment to remember. "Albert. Albert Dance."

"I'm Eve," she said. "I need your help but it will hurt."

"Where?"

"Everywhere, but it will pass and you must not scream. Do you understand? They will hear if you scream."

You tried to tell her that you couldn't scream if you wanted, but all you could manage was a weak, "Yes."

She flicked a switch on the machine then tugged the wires and tubes from your body. She was right. The pain left no part of you untouched. You swallowed your agony and it passed. You sat up in your bed. "Why does it hurt so much?"

"The one in the back of the neck is called an incapacitator. When it comes out, all the pain it has numbed floods back in one go. At least you had warning. The big nurse with the limp disconnected my incapacitator by accident," she said.

"What's wrong with us?" you asked.

"This place is what's wrong with us."

"But isn't all this supposed to make us better?"

"Do you feel any better?"

"I don't know. I'm not sure what was wrong in the first place. I didn't have any symptoms."

"Nor did I."

You glanced back at the rest of the room. "Why me?"

"Why any of us?" replied Eve.

"I mean, why did you choose to save me?"

"I thought I'd stand a better chance of getting out if there were two of us and you were the nearest to my bed. In a minute, the night nurse will open that door to do her round. That will be our chance. The door is locked but if we hide behind the desk, we can slip through before she spots us. Then we run."

"Run?" you said. "I'm not sure I can walk."

With Eve's help, you got out of the bed and followed her to the desk. It was strange to be on your feet again. You felt like a toddler who had only just learned how to stand. Somehow you made it to the desk when your eyes fell on a newspaper with a circled advert.

WANTED: Healthy unwanted children
for important experimentation.
Financial compensation paid upon delivery.
Contact Doctor Finbar Good,
Larkin Mills Department of Progress

"Quick, she's coming." Eve grabbed your sleeve and dragged you down behind the desk.

The door opened but the nurse stopped, gasped and closed it again.

"What happened?" you asked.

"She must have seen the empty beds." You could hear the frustration in Eve's voice. "We'll have to return and make it look like we never left. She's the one who drinks so they won't believe her if we reattach all the tubes."

"Reattach the tubes." You tasted the horror of those words. "I can't."

"You can and you have to if you are to get out. All except the incapacitator. Just tuck that behind your neck. We'll try again tomorrow night."

You both went back to your beds and reinserted the tubes. It was even worse than you imagined it would be. Unspeakably painful. You got the last one in, just in time.

The night nurse returned with Doctor Good. You heard her telling him that the beds had been empty, but she couldn't remember which ones. He sniffed her breath. "I think you had better take the rest of the evening off," he said. "In the morning I will talk to your superior about having you moved to the terminal toenail unit."

"But, I swear . . . "

"Good night, sister," said Doctor Good.

You spent the rest of the night lying in the bed, trying to understand what was happening. You found you could think more clearly with the incapacitator unplugged. It made sleep impossible, and being awake unbearable. You thought about that advert in the newspaper on the desk. You wondered whether it was possible that you were an unwanted child. All night you watched the nurses come in and out, with the precision of prison guards. It was getting light outside when two of them stopped by your bed.

"I hate this ward," said one.

"At least it's quiet. You know Julie down in the hospice? She says she's run off her feet."

"I'd do anything to work down there. This place gives me the creeps."

Both nurses' gazes drifted to you. You remained still.

"Come on," said the other. "Let's go and have a cup of tea. This lot aren't going anywhere. That program you like is on in a minute."

"The one in which those hypnotized people are made to eat sandpaper?"

"No. The one where the contestants are told their families are dead."

"Oh, I love that one. It's so funny."

When you come to tell this anecdote, you may question whether some of its elements seem a little too contrived. Why was the tell-tale newspaper article lying there on the nurse's desk? Why did these two gossiping nurses stop by your bed? Do not worry about these details. All good anecdotes require minor corrections. The details may have been tweaked but the essence of the story is true.

4.

That next night, you waited for Eve to move before beginning the painful process of removing the wires and tubes. It was no easier the second time. You prayed there would not be a third.

"I've been thinking about what to do," said Eve when she joined you. "Our beds are too near the doors to be left empty – they'll get spotted again. But the beds go all the way back along the ward. We just need to wheel two from down there over here, so that when the night nurse comes in she doesn't notice immediately that we're gone."

"But she'll still notice eventually."

"Maybe, but we'll have bought ourselves some time."

You followed Eve into the depths of the gloomy room. The sound of your footsteps echoed off the walls, adding rhythm to the beeping machines. In the darkest corner, you located two beds: one with a boy, one with a girl.

"We'll have to unplug the tubes to move them, then reconnect them at the other end," said Eve. "The beds are on wheels so it shouldn't take long."

"I'm not sure I can do it," you replied.

"You have to," she said. "Our eyes are open now. We must escape this evil so we can stop it."

You knew she was right. You looked at the boy, fast asleep in the bed. You pulled out his tubes but he didn't react until you reached the one at the back of his neck. He gasped and stared at you with sickening fear, trying to speak but unable. He was petrified.

"Trust me," you said.

He did. He knew that you were here to help him.

You quickly wheeled him across the ward and tried to remain behind him but you could see him twitching, trying to look back at you. One of the wheels squeaked and refused to go in the right direction. You got him to your spot and pushed the bed into place. The only way of reconnecting the incapacitator was to lift his head. When you did, you were forced to look into his terrified eyes.

"Why?" he gasped.

"Come on," urged Eve. She had already reconnected her replacement.

"Why?" repeated the boy, his right hand grasping the sleeve of your dressing gown.

"I have no choice," you replied as you thrust that tube back into his neck. Were you disgusted with yourself for the relief you felt seeing the boy fall limp once more? I do not know. Some details you will need to add yourself.

Eve helped you with the other tubes and you ran back to your position behind the desk. This time, when the door opened, the night nurse didn't stop in the doorway. She walked into the ward. You and Eve made a dash for it. You made it out without being spotted. The door clicked shut behind you. As you followed her down the corridor you wondered how long it would be before your disappearance was noticed. You followed Eve into the lift and hit the button marked *Ground*. The hospital was quiet so late at night, and every door you tried was locked shut.

You suggested breaking a window but Eve pointed out they had bars on the other side. "The doors are unlocked during the day," she said. 'We'll have to hide out until then."

"But won't they notice we're gone?"

"We don't have any other choice."

You reached a door with a sign saying: *CHILDREN'S HOSPICE*.

"What's a hospice?" you asked.

"It's where they put seriously ill people. You know, the ones who aren't going to get better. It's as good a place to hide as any. No one's going to suspect anyone in a hospice of trying to walk out."

You followed her through the door into a ward full of sleeping children. You found an empty bed each and climbed in. It was your intention to stay awake but, lying in the comfortable bed with no beeping and no tubes, you fell into the deepest sleep in a long, long time. The last thing you remembered was Eve's face but, when you awoke, she was gone.

"Come on, up you get, lazy bones. It's time to go home." A smiling nurse stood over your bed.

"Home?" you said.

"That's right. It's Monday. Everyone in this ward is better now. Your parents or guardians should be at the door. Hurry up. You won't want to miss them."

"But ... " You looked at Eve's empty bed but stopped short of asking about her for fear of giving yourself away. Instead, you followed the nurse through the double doors into the bright sunlight. Its warmth brought tears to your eyes. As soon as you were out, you started to run. You didn't stop until you reached your house. You had no key so you rang the doorbell. Your mother opened the door and said, "Oh, you're back, are you? Finished with you, have they? Well, you'd better go upstairs and change. You can't hang around in those hospital clothes, darling dear. I have the Society Against Unwelcome Visitors coming round shortly. We're trying to stop the steam fair using the park. Those people are a law unto themselves. Have a bath while you're there. You reek. Don't they wash you in the hospital?"

You went upstairs and got changed into clothes that no longer fitted. You had grown taller but got thinner. The next day your mother told you to pack your things because you were moving house.

5.

Albert stared open-mouthed at the salesman. "I don't understand," he said.

"Which aspect? Why your mother was willing to sacrifice you? What happened to Eve? How did Doctor Good avoid conviction? How could you forget all this? How it is you remember now?"

"Yes. All of that. As you told the story, it all came back to me. I even remember my mother saying we were moving house, but we never did."

"So I see." The salesman looked around at the Room for Best.

"What were they doing to us?"

17

"Doctor Good won a number of awards for his work with terminally ill children. No matter what they had, he succeeded where others had failed. The truth is that he wasn't curing illness. He was redistributing it. All those wires and tubes that were inside you. They were not to make you feel better. They were sucking out your good health and feeding it into the dying. We were unwanted healthy children being used to help unhealthy wanted children."

"We?"

The salesman removed his glasses.

Albert looked into his eyes and understood. "You were the boy in the bed. The one I moved."

The salesman nodded. "The one who trusted you."

"I'm sorry." Albert's voice wavered with fear. "I never knew."

"Don't worry," said the salesman, with a comforting smile. "I'm not here for revenge. We both know where the blame lies."

"Doctor Good?"

"An evil enough man, yes, but what of those who delivered us to him? Those parents and guardians who traded us all in?"

"I am not the first you have spoken to, am I?" said Albert.

"No. I have been tracking down surviving patients from that wing for many years. It has not been easy. The remaining victims, myself included, were released when the hospital was shut down after that virus spread from a trashy science fiction story. All the records were destroyed, but I have ways of finding people."

"Are there many more survivors?"

"Yes, but not all as blissfully unaware as you were." The salesman pushed his glasses up his nose. "I have witnessed horrors beyond nightmares. I have met people whose health was irrecoverably extracted, leaving them freakishly disfigured."

"But why?" asked Albert. "Why are you doing this?"

"My employer likes to see people get their just desserts in this life."

"Your employer?"

"Albert. Don't worry about my role in this. This anecdote is yours. All it is lacking in an ending."

"An ending?"

Upstairs, Mrs. Dance banged on the floor. Albert looked down at the glass of whiskey on the sideboard. The salesman caught his eye and Albert saw that he was still holding a small vial of deep purple liquid. He pulled off the top and held it out.

"Albert, darling dear, bring my medicine. I need my medicine," yelled Mrs. Dance.

"It will be painless," said the salesman. "It's more than she deserves."

"There's so much I need to understand," said Albert.

"There's only one question you need to ask," responded the salesman. "Why?" he asked. "Why?"

Albert remembered the answer he had given before. "I have no choice," he replied. He picked up the whiskey and held it out so the salesman could pour in the contents. Then he called out, "Coming now, Mother. I'm coming with your medicine."

The Removal Men

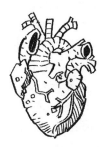

1.

IVOR FELT HONORED to be sitting in the passenger seat of his mother's car. As mayor of Larkin Mills, Mrs. Kendall was terribly busy so she usually sent one of her 'people' to collect him from school.

"It's nice of you to pick me up," he said.

"Your aunt Morwenna is at home," replied his mother. "I need you to promise to be on your best behavior."

"Who is Aunt Morwenna?" Ivor had never heard the name before.

"She is my sister."

"You have a sister?"

"Please try not to touch the dashboard, darling. I've only just had it polished. And of course I have a sister. I've alluded to her on several occasions."

"Have you?"

Mrs. Kendall cleared her throat, in the way she always did before public speeches. "On the third of March, during a public address by *The Big Heart*, at which you were present, I used a plural first person pronoun twice when recalling a story concerning my childhood, a clear indication that I have a sibling."

"I ... er ... " Mayor Kendall was a famously brilliant debater. Ivor never stood a chance in disagreements.

"Paragraph four, line two, and I quote: Larkin Mills was a much safer place when *we* were young. *We* could play in the streets without fear and such is my vision of the future. Under my leadership, I will bring a new era of mass civil obedience ... A unified town under one protective roof."

Ivor didn't think it sounded like the most obvious reference to his aunt but he knew better than to argue his case. "Where has she been until now?"

"She's been away. Now, please, I need to listen to the news. There's a report on a young doctor who is making big waves in the world of medicine. Doctor Good is one of the rising stars of the Larkin Mills Department of Planning."

When they arrived home, Mrs. Kendall went to iron the doilies and bleach the salt crystals in preparation for dinner while Ivor went into the drawing room to introduce himself to his aunt, who was sitting on the settee, catching teardrops in a teacup.

"You must be Ivor," said Morwenna. "I've heard so much about you."

"Have you?" said Ivor, unable to say the same.

"Yes. I'm looking forward to getting to know you now I'm back in Larkin Mills."

"Where will you live?" Ivor very much hoped she wasn't

going to move into his house. Whenever visitors stayed with them, his mother always gave them his room and made him sleep in the attic. He hated it up there. He always banged his head on the low ceiling and woke up sneezing from the dust.

"I'm going to be moving into your dear departed grandmother's house."

"But Grandma's not dead," he said.

"No, but she is dear, and she will be departed when they come to take her to the Home for the Extremely Inactive this evening. Once she has gone, I shall move back in."

"Back in?" said Ivor.

"Yes, I used to live there before I went *away*."

"Where did you go?" Ivor asked.

Aunt Morwenna looked at him with an expression that shifted from sadness to fear before settling on self-pity with a touch of tragedy.

"You never met my husband, did you? Your uncle Dulwich was a good man. Generous to a fault. If he was here now he'd, most likely, reach into his pocket and give you a pound just for being his nephew." Aunt Morwenna fiddled with her handbag then pulled out a shiny coin. She blew the dust off it then dropped it back inside. "Yes, Dulwich West was a wonderful man in so many ways."

"How did he die?"

Aunt Morwenna had barely stopped crying throughout the conversation but she reacted to this question with a howl of agony and a tidal wave of tears. Ivor's mother entered the room.

"Ivor," she scolded. "You've upset your aunt."

She sat down next to her sister and placed an arm around her shoulder. "I'm sorry. He's only a child. He knows no better."

"It's not his fault," replied Morwenna. "I know I should have got over it by now but the wound still feels so fresh."

"Morwenna, Dulwich vanished a long time ago." Ivor's mother adopted the tone she used when she thought Ivor was making a fuss about nothing. "You need to move on with your life. Are you sure about staying at Mother's? You can stay here for as long as you like. You can sleep in Ivor's room. He's quite happy in the attic."

Ivor's heart sank.

"That's kind of you, but no," said Aunt Morwenna.

"But all those memories." Ivor's mother picked up Morwenna's teacup and wiped underneath it.

"I'm not afraid of memories. It's forgetting that I fear."

"Sometimes one must forget the things we don't have, to remember those things we do."

Ivor's mother patted her sister's hand. She often concluded conversations with statements that sounded cleverer than they were. It was a technique that worked well during public debates because, by the time the other person had worked out what she meant, she had moved on.

2.

Morwenna moved into Grandma's house later that evening. Ivor felt sorry for his grandmother having to go into a home but he was pleased to have his aunt out of the house. Once she had gone, Ivor's mother suggested they dust the top of the kitchen door as a bit of a treat. Ivor didn't really share his mother's passion for cleaning but he didn't want to offend her so went to find the cleaning sponges and a footstool.

"What was Morwenna's husband like?" he asked, watching

his mother run a damp sponge across the top of the door.

"Your uncle Dulwich was a concrete artist. He didn't earn very much money, which was why they lived with Grandma," replied Mrs. Kendall.

"A concrete artist?" said Ivor.

"Yes. It used to be all the rage until the bottom dropped out of the market. Hold the stool steady, please. I'm going to try to do the coving while I'm up here." She had to stand on tiptoes to reach.

"You did the coving last week," said Ivor.

"The struggle against dust is a war not a battle. A neverending war," said Mrs. Kendall.

"So what happened to Dulwich?" asked Ivor.

His mother sighed. "One day Morwenna returned home to find he had vanished. She has been searching for him all this time."

"So he's not dead?" said Ivor.

"He's as good as dead," replied his mother.

"As good as dead?"

"Yes. Without finding a body, one can only be declared as good as dead. It's one of those old by-laws that date back to goodness knows when. Just like the one about driving on the right on the ring road."

"So Dulwich might be alive?" he said.

His mother stepped off the stool and handed the sponge to Ivor. "No. People don't come back from being as good as dead any more than they come back from the dead."

"So how was he declared as good as dead?"

"I pulled in a favor and had the certificate drawn up." Ivor's mother never tired of reminding Ivor what an important and influential person she was as mayor. "It's usually a very costly business but Mr. Milkwell is a close personal friend of mine."

"Mr. Milkwell, the undertaker?"

"And hotelier, yes. I know him well. He does a lot of work for us. I had Dulwich declared as good as dead as a kindness to your aunt. Morwenna wearing black is a sign she is finally coming to terms with the fact that he has gone for good. Mourning is a step forward. She is vanquishing any remaining hope that he might one day return, which he mostly certainly will not."

"Has she really been looking for him all this time?"

His mother walked to the cutlery drawer and pulled out a bread knife. She grinned at Ivor. "What do you say? Shall we have a late one and get the knives gleaming?"

"I suppose," he said. "How long ago was all this?"

"Dulwich vanished fifteen years ago," said his mother.

"Fifteen years?" exclaimed Ivor. "If she hasn't got over it in fifteen years what makes you think she will now?"

Mrs. Kendall placed the knife she was holding back inside the drawer and put down her polishing rag. Ivor had offended her. "Perhaps we should call it a night after all."

"I'm sorry," he said.

"Morwenna is family and we never give up on family. No matter what. One must help those under our own roof, whatever the situation."

3.

Ivor was hopeful that his mother would pick him up the following day but, when the mirrored window lowered, it was her driver, Finchley, at the wheel.

"Good afternoon, Master Kendall." Ivor had never seen

Finchley's face properly because of the way he wore his chauffeur's cap pulled down over his eyes.

When Ivor had asked him how he could see to drive like that, the chauffeur had replied, without any hint that he was joking, that "I always close my eyes when I drive."

Whether or not this was true, Ivor was always grateful when the journey was over.

"Mayor Kendall has instructed me to take you to your grandmother's house," said Finchley. "She says you are to wait there until she comes to collect you."

Ivor took his place in the passenger seat and pulled on his seatbelt. "Will she be late?"

"Not if she plays her cards right." A white smile appeared in the dark shadow under Finchley's visor.

"Is it a debate or something?"

"More like a coup. Larkin Mills is about to undergo a power shift but, with your mother's survival instincts, I'm sure she will ride this storm and come out on top." Finchley started the car and pulled out so suddenly that another car had to swerve. As usual, Ivor was unable to see whether his eyes were open or shut, but the journey was as hair-raisingly terrifying as usual. Finchley dropped Ivor off outside his grandmother's house. "Your mother has asked me to remind you to keep to light subjects and avoid any mention of you know what."

"I'll try," said Ivor but it was easier said than done.

Morwenna was crying when she opened the front door. "I'm sorry." She dabbed her eyes with a white handkerchief embroidered with blue and yellow flowers. "I was chopping onions."

"Mum says if you cut them under water they don't make you cry," said Ivor, following her in.

"I did do that," said Aunt Morwenna. "It wasn't the onions

27

that made me cry. It's just that Dulwich always used to chop the onions."

"What are you making?" asked Ivor, in an attempt to steer the conversation to safer territory.

"A Spanish omelette." She sobbed. "I'm sorry. It's just that Dulwich and I honeymooned in Spain."

Ivor wondered what happened if you cried too much. Could you run out of tears? Could you cry yourself dry? Was there a danger that Aunt Morwenna might end up shrivelled like a self-pitying prune? Maybe she drank all that tea to keep herself hydrated. She managed to down twelve cups during the short time he was there. She didn't offer Ivor anything. They sat in the lounge with the television switched off, while Aunt Morwenna drank, sniffed, wept and talked incessantly about her ex-husband.

"Mum told me he was declared as good as dead," Ivor said.

"Yes, it was a kindness of your mother to do that," said Morwenna. "She's a very important person, you know."

"But if they never found the body, there's hope that he's alive, isn't there?"

"You say that like it's a good thing," said Aunt Morwenna.

"Wouldn't it be a good thing?"

"His As Good As Death certificate gives me tremendous comfort." She opened her purse and pulled out an envelope. From within, this she pulled out a letter and unfolded it. Ivor had once heard that it was impossible to fold a piece of paper more than seven times but he lost count of how many times Aunt Morwenna unfolded this one. When she finished she passed it to him.

"Did he have a will or estate?" asked Ivor.

Morwenna shook her head sadly. "Money wasn't Dulwich's strong point. He was an artist."

"A concrete artist?" said Ivor.

"Yes." For a moment Aunt Morwenna's eyes lit up with something that resembled happiness. "Back when I married him, concrete art was all the thing. Every art gallery in the country was buying concrete artworks and Larkin Mills was leading the way. Larkin Mills National Museum was full of them. In the right hands, concrete was worth its weight in gold, and Dulwich's hands were masterly. He could make things out of concrete that would make you weep. He made *The Big Heart*. It was Dulwich's finest work."

"Uncle Dulwich made *The Big Heart*?" said Ivor, impressed.

Everyone in Larkin Mills knew *The Big Heart*. It was a landmark, slap bang in the middle of the town square. It was a huge anatomically accurate human heart with water running through its arteries and shooting out of its sides. It was one of those things that people met by. In the summer, children splashed around in the water that collected at its base. In the winter, people who had drunk too much balanced Christmas hats on top of it. All year round, pigeons used it for target practice. Ivor had heard his mother describe it as the living soul of Larkin Mills.

"He must have got paid a lot for that," said Ivor.

"Yes, well. The council commissioned it when concrete was all the rage. They paid him half his fee up front but he spent all that on materials and paying off debts. By the time it was ready, concrete had fallen out of fashion so they refused to pay the rest. I suppose Dulwich couldn't live with the rejection."

"So how did it end up in the square?"

"The council said that since their money had been used to pay for the concrete, the statue belonged to them. It has been in the square ever since."

"But they never paid the full amount?"

"I suppose not," said Aunt Morwenna with a look that said, *That is hardly the point.* "But at least Dulwich's work didn't go to waste."

"So when did he vanish?"

"It was his last day working on the piece. He was busy in his studio – or so I believed. I took the phone call from the council saying they weren't going to pay. I went to tell him but, when I got there, he was gone."

"So he never learned that the council were refusing to pay."

Aunt Morwenna shrugged. "Maybe someone had already told him. I can't remember if there was a phone in the studio." She paused to think. "So much of it is a blur now. It's funny the things you do and don't remember. I've gone over the events of that day so many times, hoping to find a clue, and the only thing I can remember clearly was the removal van parked outside that day. I think it stuck in my memory because of the name. Complete Removals. I suppose poor Dulwich was completely removed, wasn't he?"

"Do you think this van was involved?"

"No. I asked your mother. She said it's just a removal company. They have vans going all over town, apparently."

"Did you try calling them? I mean, what if they had something to do with Uncle Dulwich's disappearance? What if they saw something?"

"No, your mother says it's nothing. Dulwich is gone and that is that."

Aunt Morwenna folded the letter again and dropped it into the envelope.

It was typical that Ivor's mother arrived just at the point Ivor's aunt was becoming interesting. She let herself in, marched into the living room and demanded to know what they were talking about.

"Ivor was telling me about his day at school," said Morwenna.

"Good. Come on, Ivor. If we go now we'll still have time to bleed the radiators and scrub the bathroom tiles."

"Goodbye, Ivor, dear," said Morwenna. "Thank you for listening."

Aunt Morwenna closed the door and Ivor followed his mother to the car. He sat down in the passenger seat and Mrs. Kendall started the engine.

"Why did your aunt thank you for listening?" she said. "What was she telling you?"

"About the removal van," said Ivor.

"Oh, not this again," his mother replied. "I've told you. It's an ordinary removal company and no one saw what happened to Dulwich. It was all thoroughly investigated a long time ago."

"What if they were in on it?" asked Ivor.

"Complete Removals is a reputable company. The council used them last year after we had that decomposing problem with the walls. They were very efficient. Now, please, no more of this nonsense."

"But ... "

"No more," snapped his mother. "Your aunt requires our love and support, not some kind of misjudged junior investigation."

4.

Ivor would have left it at that had he not spotted the Complete Removals van across the road while helping his mother clean the curtain rails. It stopped outside the Dances' house. The driver, who wore orange overalls, took a heavy-looking piece of equipment from the back of the van and carried it into the house while Mrs. Dance held the door open for him. Ivor knew Mrs. Dance, whose lemonade was a big hit with the adults during the garden party season, and who always used the opportunity to bend Ivor's mother's ear about her latest cause. Apparently she had a son called Albert but Ivor had never seem him because, according to his mother, he was a sickly child and had spent most of his childhood in the hospital.

"Are the Dances moving house?" he asked, trying not to drop the curtain rings she was passing to him.

"I don't think so. Why?" replied his mother.

"There's a removal van outside," he said.

His mother looked out of the window. "It's very rude to spy on one's neighbors," she said.

"Sorry."

When he had sponged the final curtain ring he asked, "Can I go out and play in the garden now?"

"Yes, I suppose," said his mother. "So long as you do the skirting boards before bed."

Ivor went to investigate. In the books he liked reading, children were always investigating mysterious goings on. There were ups and downs in these adventures but things tended to end pretty well. Surely writers wouldn't be allowed to write such things if they weren't true, he thought.

After three circuits around the van Ivor was disappointed by the lack of conveniently overheard conversations or well-placed clues that his reading had led him to expect. Then he remembered how the heroes in his books usually put themselves in dangerous situations and, as a consequence, often learned a vital clue. Ivor had shimmied up a lamppost and climbed on top of the van when he heard the front door open.

"Thank you so much," said Mrs. Dance.

"Just doing my job," replied the man. "Give me a call if you have any problems."

"What kind of problems?" asked Mrs. Dance.

"There is a list of the possible side-effects in the pamphlet, but I really wouldn't worry. They print a lot of that stuff to cover their backs. Your son took to the process very well. When you've done this job as long as me, you get to know the problem patients. Albert will be fine."

"Oh, well, thank you," replied Mrs. Dance. "I wouldn't want anything to happen to my darling dear. He's been sickly all his life."

"Well, that's all in the past now." The door closed and the man got back into the van. Ivor realized he had two options now. Either he could reveal his presence and explain what he was doing on top of the van or he could find something to cling onto and brace himself. Again, he thought about the book characters who put themselves in peril and survived. He remained on top of the van.

The short journey was surprisingly painful and unbelievably terrifying. By the time the van stopped outside a warehouse, Ivor had sworn never to do anything so stupid again. Seeing a uniformed woman step out of a booth, Ivor ducked down.

"Afternoon, Brian," she said. "You dropping off?"

"Yep."

"Name?"

"Dance."

The women checked her list. "Yes. That's fine."

"You don't mind if I leave the van inside over lunch, do you? The parking round here is terrible. Last time I left the van on a yellow line for an hour it cost me three months' wages."

"You buying lunch?" said the woman, picking up her coat.

"You've twisted my arm. I'll file this one when I get back then." He parked the van inside and locked the warehouse door.

Ivor slipped off the top and opened the back door of the van. Inside was a cardboard box marked with a large red letter D. Inside, he found a paper dressing gown, a pile of books and a medical tag with the name *Dance, Albert* written on it. He replaced the lid and closed the van door. The warehouse was full of identical cardboard boxes, each with a letter written on the side. He checked a couple of these and found they contained photographs, letters, ornaments and clothes. Ivor was confused. Why would a removals firm lock up all this stuff?

The letters were arranged alphabetically so Ivor had to walk the full length of the warehouse to find the 'W' section. He rooted through a few boxes until he found one labelled 'West' that included a wedding photograph of Aunt Morwenna and a dark-haired man. There was a newspaper article with a picture of the same man. *BRIGHT NEW FACE IN CONCRETE* read the headline. Below this was a biography of Dulwich West and a piece about his work. The next article proudly proclaimed, *A NEW HEART FOR LARKIN MILLS*. This one included an interview with Uncle Dulwich about the project. A third headline read, *BOTTOM DROPS OUT OF CONCRETE ART MARKET*.

Ivor was halfway through it when he heard approaching footsteps. He hastily placed everything back in the box and ducked out of sight. The door opened. Another man in orange overalls entered, carrying a box. He left the door ajar behind him. Ivor wanted to learn more but not at the cost of getting trapped inside the warehouse. He took the opportunity, slipped out, ran to the road and caught a bus home.

5.

In Ivor's books, the junior investigators often had a good reason not to tell their parents about the sinister plots they had uncovered, but Ivor could think of no reason not to tell his mother. Mayor Kendall mixed with important people. She had the home numbers of police commissioners, magistrates and judges. If Complete Removals really was removing people, Ivor's mother could have them investigated.

That evening at the dining table, Ivor told his mother all that he had learned about the suspicious behavior of Complete Removals, although he left out some of the more dangerous details of his investigation. They were eating linguine, although it was taking a long time as his mother was insisting that they each clean and polish the silverware in-between each mouthful. She listened politely until he had finished.

"One thing is for sure. You have strengthened my resolve to outlaw all junior investigations," she said. "It will be against the law for anyone under the age of sixteen to follow anyone, come up with outlandish theories or overhear conveniently placed conversations."

"You must admit that it is odd, though," said Ivor. "All that stuff in the warehouse."

Ivor's mother carefully cleaned her fork with a damp sponge, then picked up a polishing cloth. "These newspaper articles you read. They mentioned Dulwich's disappearance, did they?"

"Yes."

"But nothing about what happened to him?"

"I thought you said no one knew what happened to him."

His mother held the polished fork up to the light to check it was pristine before using it to twizzle the next piece of pasta. "Since you seem so set on pushing this, I will tell you. Your uncle was murdered."

"Murdered?"

"Yes. Had you not been interrupted in your ridiculous investigation, you would have read further articles in which your aunt was at first suspected, and later convicted of the murder of Dulwich."

"Aunt Morwenna killed Uncle Dulwich?"

"I don't know why you insist on repeating everything I say, but yes. Aunt Morwenna murdered your uncle."

"Why?"

"Both of us were ambitious but, unlike me, she wanted to

make her money through marriage. I warned her against the unpredictability of marrying an artist but she didn't listen. She believed concrete art was a solid investment. It was not. It was already showing cracks when they married. When the bottom fell out of the market, the only artworks of any value were those made by dead artists."

"So how did she kill him?"

Ivor's mother picked up a fresh grater and sprinkled a little Parmesan over her dinner. She carried the grater to the sink, washed it, dried it and returned to the table. "On the day I informed her that the council would not be paying the remaining amount for its commission, she pushed him into the mold of his final piece of work."

"*The Big Heart?*"

"*The Big Heart.*"

Ivor felt a confusing mix of revulsion and intrigue. "Did they find him inside?"

"There was no need. Morwenna had confessed and, since *The Big Heart* was an official commission with an increased value after Dulwich's death, it was decided best to take her word for it and leave the piece intact."

"But the council never paid the full amount."

"Honestly, Ivor," said his mother. "I'm not going to sit here discussing council decisions made over a decade ago."

"So Uncle Dulwich's dead body is inside *The Big Heart* in the middle of the town square just rotting away?" Ivor was unable to hide his horror.

"Everything has to be somewhere," said his mother plainly. "Some dead bodies are buried in the cemetery, some are bricked up behind walls. There are probably some still lingering in the reservoir. Your uncle is in the town square. You've

37

missed a smudge on the back of your fork, dear."

Ivor picked up the polishing cloth and cleaned the fork. "Did she go to prison?"

"Of course. That's where she's been all this time, in prison for the murder of your uncle."

"You mean that she's just pretending that he vanished?"

"Pretending? No, she's not pretending. Morwenna believes what she says."

"But how can she?"

"Morwenna was released from prison last week. She had served her time. I felt that she had suffered enough so I called in a favor and had her memories removed."

"You did what?"

"Complete Removals don't remove objects. They remove memories. They have an extractor thing. I don't know how it works, something to do with targeting the part of your brain where the memory is, then removing it. Of course, they have to take all those items that might trigger any memories too. That's what you found in that box."

"But the warehouse was full of boxes."

"Well, evidently a lot of people in this town have a lot of things they want to forget."

Ivor had lost his appetite so he carried his plate to the sink. His mother followed him.

"So Aunt Morwenna doesn't know that she is a murderer?" said Ivor.

"Oh, Ivor. Your aunt murdered *one* person. That hardly makes her a murderer. Anyway, I see now that I didn't have enough extracted. I shall call Complete Removals and have all memory of Uncle Dulwich removed entirely. So does that answer all of your questions? Can we put this matter to bed?"

"Will I still have to go round and see her?"

"Of course. Once we remove Dulwich entirely from her memories she'll need us even more. Memory is the thing that keeps us company in our solitude."

The Bargain

1.

O LIVE'S HEART SANK when she unwrapped the accordion. She could not recall a single Christmas or birthday
when she had received the present she had asked for. It wasn't
that her father was especially neglectful; he simply could not
resist a bargain.

He did all his shopping at Larkin Mills Auction House and
always prioritized a good price over the appropriateness of
the gift. The motorbike engine was a prime example. He had
acquired it at well below the estimated value but, when Olive
unwrapped it one Christmas morning, she had struggled to
find anything positive to say about it. The Russian spacesuit
was met with equal bafflement, as were the three Victorian
stuffed squirrels in ballet positions. It hadn't helped that the
squirrel performing the plié had lost its head.

The wallpaper in her room was made up of repeated pictures of professional basket weaving champions, a sport in which Olive had precisely zero interest but, as with everything else, it had been a bargain. She tried to be patient with her father. She understood that his job as a driver for a removals company wasn't well-paid but, seeing the accordion, something inside of her snapped. "Why can't you bid on something I want?" she exclaimed.

"I do," said her father. "But I never win those. That bike you wanted went sky high. With the auction commission you might as well buy one from a shop for that price."

Olive wished her father bought things from shops.

"This accordion was an absolute bargain," he enthused. "In working order, it would go for three, maybe four, times what I paid for it."

"So it's not in working order," said Olive with a heavy sigh.

"Think of it as a project."

"You mean rather than thinking of it as a broken accordion that I didn't ask for?"

"If that is your attitude, then next time I'll spend the equivalent money on a toy that will lose its value the moment you take it out of its box."

"Yes, that's what I want!" exclaimed Olive.

"Then maybe that's what you'll get," said her father sulkily.

Olive didn't want her father to think she was ungrateful so she said thank you for the accordion and took it upstairs to find out just how broken it was.

It was very broken. It made a wheezing sound when she pushed the two sides together and only the black keys worked. The case was missing a strap and refused to shut properly. Olive considered herself a positive person and had developed a

42

genuine affection for her mismatched collection of objects, but it was difficult to see the value of an unplayable instrument.

"What do you think, Madame Amuse-Bouche?" she asked the least flea-bitten stuffed squirrel. "Should I repair it?"

As an only child, Olive often named and talked to the objects in her room. She picked up the pirouetting squirrel and, in her Victorian squirrel voice, said, "Olive, my girl, you should repair it at once."

The squirrel was right. The previous Christmas Olive had asked for a guitar, so a musical instrument signified a step in the right direction. Perhaps her words were finally sinking in.

"Hey there, Monkey." Her father popped his head around the bedroom door. "Our program is about to start."

"I'll be down in a minute," said Olive.

Flog It Or Burn It was her father's latest obsession. It involved competitors trying to sell their family heirlooms against the clock, the twist being that the person who had the most unsold items when the time ran out was forced to burn their remaining things in front of a live studio audience. When Olive had first watched it, she had worried that it was cruel but her father had explained that TV contestants knew what they were getting into and only got what they deserved. His favorite bit was the end of the show, when they showed a close up of the box of matches just before the unfortunate losers were forced to watched their prized possessions reduced to ash.

"Come on, Olive," called her father. "The music's starting."

She pushed the heavy accordion between a set of deep-sea diving bellows and a mahogany-mounted skeleton of a cow's leg bone, then went down to join her father.

43

As a special birthday treat, Olive's father gave her the exact money for an ice cream from Mr. Morricone's Ice Cream Parlor. She was standing in the queue outside when she spotted an advert in a newsagent's window. The advert showed no signs of age even though the shop had been closed for years.

MIGUEL'S MUSICAL REPAIRS
ANY instrument repaired.
No matter how BROKEN, Miguel will repair it.
If Miguel cannot repair it, it is beyond repair.

Marvelling at how strangely convenient it was that she should happen to read the advert just when she had a broken accordion, Olive committed the phone number to memory, then called it when she got home. After three and a half rings, someone picked up, but no one spoke.

"Hello?" said Olive. "Is that Miguel's Musical Repairs?"

"Oh right, it's that one, is it?" replied a man's voice.

"What?" It was an odd way to answer a phone.

"Nothing. This is Miguel. Who are you?"

"My name is Olive. I have a broken accordion."

"Right. And?"

"I was wondering how much it would cost to fix it," she said.

"Are you sure you want it fixed?"

"I think so." Olive thought this an especially strange conversation.

"Excellent, then bring it in." The man's voice brightened. "My shop is on the corner of Hansler Road, the next bus stop on from the pet gymnasium, or just off the ring road if you're driving. It's one of the top five accident hot spots in the whole country." He sounded very much like he was boasting about this fact.

There were no other musical instrument repair shops in Larkin Mills so Olive strapped the case shut using a pair of her father's braces and lugged it out of the house. It was a pain to carry and it seemed to grow heavier with each step. She couldn't get a seat on the bus as it was rammed full of people with fat pets. There were tubby dogs, chubby cats and portly gerbils. Olive was pushed up against a goldfish bowl containing an extremely unfit-looking goldfish. Whenever the bus took a corner too fast, the water lapped over the top of the bowl and splashed Olive.

The window of Miguel's Musical Repairs was full of all kinds of musical instruments. The sign said *OPEN* so she pushed the door. It was attached to a mechanism that dragged a bow across a viola. It made an awful screeching noise. A tall, skinny man with dark eyes, white teeth and a tin helmet with two trumpet horns sticking out of the top was talking to a man in a grey suit, sucking on a rolled-up leaf. They stood on either side of a desk with legs made from various woodwind instruments.

"Sorry." The man in the helmet addressed her. "I've been meaning to get the door-viola tuned. How can I help you?"

"I'm Olive. I called earlier about the accordion."

"Then you are a perfect excuse to get rid of this tiresome salesman. I'm Miguel."

"I'll take my leave then, shall I?" The other man dropped the soggy leaf on the floor and stamped on it.

Miguel pulled out a small bottle of purple liquid. "Don't forget the valve oil you came in for."

"Thank you." The suited man took the bottle and popped

it into his briefcase. As he walked out of the shop, he glanced down at Olive. "Take my advice and be clear about what you want before you sign anything," he said.

The viola made another awful sound as the salesman left.

"What was he selling?" she asked.

"Resolutions. But let us not dwell on endings. You are here for a new beginning. Let's get the patient on the slab, then."

Olive lifted the accordion onto the desk. It was gloomy inside the shop so Miguel switched on a lamp made from a bassoon. When he opened up the case, the bright light reflected on the velvet lining and made his face glow red. He held his hands above the instrument as though it was the most precious thing he had ever seen.

"Lovely." He pulled on a pair of white gloves. "Lovely." Miguel adjusted his helmet and lifted the accordion with the tenderness of one picking up a newborn baby. As he pulled the bellows apart, the instrument made a mournful noise. "There, there, my pretty, you won't suffer long." He spoke softly to the accordion.

"Will it cost a lot to repair, because I don't have much money," said Olive. Her father had drummed into her the importance of getting an estimate of costs before entering into a contractual commitment.

"I'm sure we will be able to come to some sort of arrangement," replied Miguel.

"What sort of arrangement?" Her father had also warned against the dangers of high-interest financing schemes.

"How about this? If I repair her, you will take her to the town square every day and busk. You will soon be able to earn the money to pay me back."

"But I can't even play it," protested Olive.

"You'll learn. I'll lend you an instructional book."

"How much will I need to make?"

"The repair will cost fifty pounds."

"Fifty pounds? But that will take forever."

"I think you'll be surprised," said Miguel. "I have had other similar arrangements in the past. It is remarkable how rewarding busking in the town square can be, especially during the summer months when the steam fair is in town and so many tourists are visiting Madam Letrec's World of Wax."

Olive didn't really believe that she would raise fifty pounds playing an instrument she had never played before, but what did it matter if she failed to make enough money? He couldn't force her to keep going. Besides, it was the summer holidays and she had nothing else to do. "All right," she said. "It's a deal."

"Excellent." Miguel placed the instrument down tenderly and pulled a thick wad of yellow paper from the desk drawer. "But you must pay me every penny you earn from busking until you have paid the full amount due."

"That seems fair."

"Good. Then sign here."

He filled in Olive's name in the spaces provided and wrote £50 in the box marked *AMOUNT DUE*. "Feel free to peruse the contract at your leisure," he said.

Olive's father had told her never to sign anything she hadn't read but this was extremely long and very boring. The first few pages were taken up by a list of the various instruments the contract covered. In total it was over twenty pages long and every inch of it was filled with unreadably dull legal jargon.

"Why is it so long?" asked Olive.

"It's a standard contact. Lots of legal mumbo-jumbo. In the good old days one did these things on a handshake but you know how strict these things are now."

"I suppose."

Olive signed her name under Miguel's squiggle. "When should I come back to collect the accordion?"

"Collect? She's good as new." Miguel pushed the bellows together, producing a melancholy chord, then moved his fingers across the keyboard to play a pretty melody.

"But that took no time to fix at all." As far as Olive could tell, Miguel had barely touched the instrument.

"I can break her just as quickly." Miguel smiled warmly. "Anyone else in my field would take twice as long and charge you three times as much for an instrument that worked half as well. I've also fixed your case and attached straps to make it easier to carry."

He handed the instrument to Olive.

"Try her for yourself."

Olive pressed down on the keys and felt a sharp pain in her finger. "Ow." She pulled it away. A droplet of blood fell from her finger and landed on the contract. It spread like an inkblot on the thick yellow paper. Miguel picked it up, blew on it to dry it, and dropped it back into the drawer.

"My apologies," he said. "I thought that key was a little sharp. Allow me."

He took the accordion off her, made a couple of adjustments then placed it back inside the case and snapped it shut.

"What about the book?" asked Olive.

"It's already inside." He opened the case again to reveal a small book lying on top called *How to Play the Accordion for Love and Money*.

In spite of the oddness of the encounter, Olive did like the idea of learning a skill that would be both enjoyable and profitable so she put aside any questions she had and picked up the accordion case.

"I look forward to your first repayment," said Miguel.

3.

Olive spent the journey home studying the manual and the rest of the day in her bedroom trying to get to grips with the instrument. Miguel was right about the book. There were clear diagrams and helpful tips. Olive had no formal musical training but, by the end of the day, she had got to grips with the first basic sea shanty. To begin with, her father was delighted that she was using the present but, as she played the same tune over and over, it began to grate on his nerves.

He popped his head around the side of her bedroom door. "Don't your fingers get tired?" he asked.

"No, they're fine. Listen." She played the tune again.

He smiled thinly. "That is excellent, but our program is about to start."

Olive would rather have stayed practicing but she understood that it was more fun to watch the show with someone else, so she put away the accordion and joined her father downstairs.

It was too late to practice by the time *Flog It Or Burn It* had finished but, first thing the next morning, Olive picked up the accordion and continued where she had left off. She didn't stop until her bleary-eyed father came in. "Olive, honey. You woke me up."

"Sorry. Haven't you got work today, though?"

"No jobs on today," he said. "Would you mind doing your practice in the park?"

"The steam fair is there at the moment."

"The town center, then. You never know, some kind soul may take pity on you and throw you a coin."

"To make me stop playing," she joked.

"No, no, no," said her father. "It's a lovely noise. It's just that I'm trying to sleep."

Olive packed up the accordion and left. It was early when she arrived at the square so she pretty much had the place to herself. She sat down by *The Big Heart*, opposite Madam Letrec's World of Wax, and began working her way through the exercises and melodies in the book. Olive was so absorbed in what she was doing, she barely noticed it get busier around her. She almost jumped out of her skin when something landed in the accordion case. She stopped and leaned forward to see what it was. A shiny pound coin lay in the case. She picked it up.

"Don't stop." An elderly lady stood in front of her. She wore a black shawl. "It's a lovely instrument. It reminds me of the time I visited Madrid with ... " Her eyes glazed over and a tear fell down her cheek. She wiped her eyes with a handkerchief embroidered with blue and yellow flowers. "I'm sorry, I get so confused these days. I'm not even sure if I've been to Madrid. Perhaps it was Paris ... but you do play very nicely."

"Thank you," said Olive.

More money was thrown into the case that day. At one point, Olive stopped only to turn the page and received a small smattering of applause. Another time, a toddler danced along to the music, causing tourists to stop and take photographs. *The Big Heart* was a good spot for busking. Husbands waiting for their wives in the shops would feel guilty about standing there so long and threw money into the case. Olive learned that people were more likely to give money if she made eye contact, so she practiced playing the tunes without looking at the music.

At the end of the day she counted up the money and discovered that she had raised twenty pounds and sixty-three pence. It was almost half the total owed. At this rate her debt would be fully paid in a couple of days, then she could carry on busking and earn enough money to buy all those things her father never bought her. She retrieved a clean plastic bag from a bin to carry the money and packed up.

Miguel's shop wasn't far from the square so she decided to walk. The accordion was surprisingly light and easy to carry with its new strap. She was happily humming one of the tango pieces when she found herself on the road with Mr. Morricone's Ice Cream Parlor. It was open and yet, miraculously, there was no a queue. The plastic bag of coins weighed heavily in her hand. One ice cream wasn't going to hurt. She hadn't had a drink all day. Her throat felt dry. Why shouldn't she treat herself? Earning all that money on her first day, she deserved it. Miguel wouldn't be expecting her to have made so much money, anyway.

She went into the shop.

"It's been a busy day," said Mr. Morricone. "I'm basically wiped out. All I have left is half a tub of Mint Exodus and two scoops of Serpent's Temptation."

"I was hoping for a Chocolate Casualty," said Olive.

"I'll see what I can scrape together." Mr. Morricone glanced at her plastic bag of coins. "It looks like you've had a good day too."

"I earned it all myself," said Olive.

"I never suggested otherwise."

Mr. Morricone set about making the ice cream sundae,

explaining which sauces and sprinkles he was substituting as he went along. He warned that it wouldn't be up to his usual standard but it tasted amazing to Olive. Once her bowl was empty, she thanked the ice cream seller and continued on her way. When she arrived at Miguel's shop she found the door locked with a closed sign in the window. She knocked on it but no one answered. Olive resolved to come back the following day, and jumped on a bus home. The stop near her house was outside a mini-market so she popped in to buy a packet of crisps but ended up going for the multipack as it worked out so much cheaper per kilogram. When she reached home, she was surprised to see Miguel standing outside. Hearing her approach, he turned to face her. The street lamp came on, giving his skin a yellowish hue.

"Hello, Olive," he said. "So how did you get on?"

"Really well. Look how much I made." She handed him the bag of money.

Miguel took it off her, raised it to his ear and listened to it jingle.

"Do you know how much it is?" he asked.

"Almost twenty pounds, I think," said Olive.

"Seventeen pounds, forty-two," said Miguel. "That's a little short, isn't it?"

"For my first day?" exclaimed Olive

"Busking in the town center on a Friday, during the steam fair period. *The Big Heart's* a prime spot and you must have performed for – what? – almost seven solid hours. I'd say that would bring in something closer to twenty pounds sixty-three, wouldn't you?"

"Have you been spying on me?"

"Why? Have you been lying to me?"

"All right, I bought an ice cream and some crisps. I'll still pay you back in no time."

"Yes, but you failed to pay me the full amount you earned and on page seven of the contract it clearly states that any such failure will incur a penalty interest rate of sixty-five point sixteen per cent of the original amount." He pulled out the contract and held it up so Olive could see this written in tiny writing.

"Which means your remaining total to pay is ... " Miguel drew a pen from his top pocket and scribbled something down on the back of the contract. "Fifty pounds exactly."

"But that's not fair."

"You were happy enough to sign the contract yesterday." He folded it up and placed his pen back in his pocket.

"I promise I'll give you everything tomorrow," said Olive. "It'll be busier in town because it's the weekend and I'm getting better."

"I know you are."

"I'll pay you back."

"I know you will."

That night, Olive sat with her father watching their program and eating the crisps. They tasted stale. Olive was so annoyed she barely even noticed when a contestant fell to his knees and wept at the sight of his grandmother's beloved cuckoo clock going up in flames.

"That'll teach him," said her father. "Look at his face. What an idiot."

Olive hadn't told her father about the contract. He would only disapprove. She would deal with it herself. A couple of good days' busking by *The Big Heart* and she would be able to pay off Miguel for good.

4.

First thing the following day, Olive went to the town square. She sat down to play before the shops had even opened. By the middle of the morning she had worked her way through the book entirely. With nothing else to refer to, she composed her own tunes and improvised around the chord patterns she had learned. It was really very easy.

The combination of improved skills, an earlier start and a weekend's shopping crowd provided total earnings of fifty-one pounds and twelve pence by the end of the day. She counted it twice to check.

She had done it.

It was over.

She closed her accordion case and allowed herself a satisfied smile.

"It won't be enough."

She turned around to see who had spoken.

She was alone.

"I said it won't be enough," repeated the voice.

"Who's that? Who's there? Show yourself." She walked around the huge cement sculpture. Still no one.

"Who do you think is speaking?" asked the voice.

Olive looked into the two protruding veins of the huge concrete heart. "It's impossible. Concrete can't talk."

"Concrete? This is art. And of course art can talk. But only if the artist puts more than his heart and soul into it. He must put his whole self into it."

"That sounds like rubbish," said Olive.

"All right. Then what if an artist was pushed into his own creation by a wife who was angry with him for failing to be the man she wanted?"

"But this statue has been here for as long as I can remember. If that's true, how could you breathe? What would you eat and drink? Where would you go to the toilet?"

"There are air vents built into the structure," replied the man. "Water runs through it and there are bins near enough to reach. As for toileting, I'd rather not go into that, but, again, the holes prove useful."

Olive looked at the heart incredulously. "But it doesn't make sense. Why wouldn't you call out for help?"

"Because the only way to escape this concrete prison would be to destroy it. This is the only remaining piece of my art. I will not be its destroyer."

"So you choose to stay inside the heart?"

"Are we not all slaves to the desires of our own hearts?"

"Well, I suppose but ... "

"As the man who repaired your instrument would tell you, we are all slaves to our art."

What do you know about my deal with Miguel?" she asked.

"I know that you play your accordion very nicely," he said, "and you're appreciated at the moment, but you'll never make enough to pay him back."

"That's where you're wrong, because I already have," said Olive.

"You're mistaken. There will be some clause about the use of minor sevenths or some such nonsense. Or a shanty penalty. Or something about money earned on Saturdays not counting. He'll add on more costs and you'll owe him again tomorrow.

It will be a lower figure and you'll think it is achievable, but something will come up again and your debt will roll on and on. It will never end."

"Why do you say that?"

"Because I've seen it before. The last one had a harp. The one before that had the bagpipes. A hideous racket but lucrative enough. Well, almost. None of them ever paid him off. That's how the deal works. The contract has hundreds of clauses and loopholes. They wrap you up and bind you to him. The moment you sign your name, you are in his employ."

"He can't make me work for him if I don't want to," said Olive. "All he did was repair my accordion and lend me a book about how to play it. Once I've paid him, I'll make him tear up the contact."

"The contract is sealed with your own blood. You would live to regret any attempt to destroy it."

"How do you know all this?"

"Because I signed one too." The man inside the sculpture spoke quietly. Ashamed of himself. "I was a poor artist. The price of concrete had gone through the roof. I couldn't afford enough to create. Then I met him. He had a different name but it was him. He was a concrete dealer back then. He had a good supplier. I couldn't afford to pay him outright for what I needed so I signed one of his contracts, but I could never pay him back either. My debts grew worse and worse. Then, when the bottom fell out of the concrete art market and my dear wife saw fit to push me in here, I realized that this was my only way out of the debt."

"To hide from it."

"To disappear."

His words felt like daggers. "Is that what the harpist and the bagpiper did?" Olive asked.

"No. They went for a simpler solution. They returned their instruments."

"But ... but ... I'm so good."

"And are you not at all suspicious about that?"

"What do you mean?"

"This is your second day playing an extremely difficult instrument and yet you play it like a protégé?"

"The instructional book is very clearly written. It has these diagrams ... " Olive's words tailed off as she heard herself.

"It's all part of the deal," said the heart. "Talent, acceptance, money ... enslavement. He doesn't care about your money. He wants you in his debt and you will remain so while you keep the instrument. You are connected to him now. You must give it up. It's the only way to leave his service."

"I will not. I don't care what you say. What would you know anyway? You're just a stupid concrete artist stuck in a stupid *Big Heart*. This is my calling." Olive picked up the accordion case, threw it over her back and left. She marched fast, with her bag of money clutched in one hand. She didn't even slow down at Mr. Morricone's Ice Cream Parlor. She almost ran to Miguel's shop, but no matter how much she tried to convince herself otherwise, she knew *The Big Heart* was telling the truth. She would never be free as long as she owed Miguel for the accordion repair. She resolved to demand that he unfix it so she could get it repaired elsewhere.

There was an *OPEN* sign in the window. She pushed the door and heard a beautiful sustained note from the viola.

"Hello?" she said.

There was no reply.

57

"Miguel?" she called.

Still nothing.

It seemed strange that he should leave the shop unattended, but then, Miguel was a strange man. Olive understood that now. She decided to write him a note to go with the money, so picked up a pen from the desk. Next to it, she noticed the same brand of matchbox they used on *Flog It Or Burn It.* On the back were the words: FIRE KILLS – KEEP AWAY FROM CHILDREN.

She opened a drawer to find some paper, and spotted the contract with the dark red bloodstain and her signature. It was the only thing that proved she owed Miguel anything at all. If she destroyed it and left the money, they would be even. Dismissing the artist's warning, Olive struck a match and held it to the corner of the contract. A flame flared up so quickly that she dropped it in fright. The burning contract landed inside the drawer and the fire spread. Olive looked for something to put out the flames. She pulled out a cloth draped over a saxophone but, when she threw it on, it was even more flammable than the paper. She grabbed a bottle of the purple valve oil and squirted it at the flames but it only made matters worse. She screamed as the desk collapsed. Seeing only one way out, she grabbed the accordion case and ran.

She caught the bus by the skin of her teeth. Once it was moving, Olive calmed down. No one had seen her. No one knew she had been there. She didn't even have the money to link her to it and the contract was most definitely destroyed.

It was over.

When the bus reached her stop, she hopped off and ran home. She felt relieved. Free. She was looking forward to sitting down with her dad and watching television so she could forget all about Miguel and the contract and the man inside the concrete heart.

She half expected to find Miguel looking up at her window again and had prepared a speech but it was not he who stood on the pavement outside her house this time.

A fire truck was parked outside. Firemen held hoses, trying to get the flames under control. Olive's instincts took over. She dropped the accordion and tried to run into the house but a strong pair of arms barred her way. "You can't go in there," said a firm voice. "It's a death trap."

"But my father! My father! He's inside!"

"I'm sorry. It's too late." The fireman held her tightly and Olive watched helplessly as everything she loved went up in flames.

"It's my fault," she screamed. "I did this."

"No, it was just a terrible accident," said the fireman. "You can't blame yourself."

Olive wrestled herself free from his grip and stepped back. In her pocket, her hand found the box of matches. When the fireman was not looking she would open the accordion case, strike a match and drop it inside.

How The Roof Died

MR. MORRICONE WAS A GENIUS when it came to ice cream. Everyone said so. He did things with the stuff that we mere mortals wouldn't have dared. Bold things. Unpredictable things. Mysterious things.

His ice cream parlor was located on a quiet road just off Larkin Mills' ring road. There was no regular footfall and all other shops that opened up on the road had gone out of business after a couple of months but Mr. Morricone's Ice Cream Parlor became a destination worth seeking out. It was busiest during the summer holidays when the steam fair came to town, and straight after school, when the queue would stretch all the way down the road.

We didn't mind queuing. It gave us time to peruse the constantly changing menu. There were our favorites such as the Chocolate Knuckle Duster, the Banoffee Burial and the Treacle Torture, but it was always exciting to see what new delights had appeared. Sometimes these were created for special occasions, such as the Royal Wedding Walnut Wipe Out and the World Cup Cinnamon Catastrophe. Sometimes they were seasonal, such as the Summer Fruits Suicide or the Christmas Massacre. All of them were made with the freshest ingredients. Mr. Morricone had the widest range of cones we had ever seen, from brandy snap to dark chocolate wafer. His sauces made you feel like you were growing new taste buds. His sprinkles were delicate and exciting. But it was the ice cream that inspired a feeling beyond human emotion. We had all witnessed customers openly weeping with joy as they tasted it. We had all wept ourselves.

The parlor was popular all year round but, in the depths of winter, when the lake in the park froze over and the wind whistled mournfully through *The Big Heart*, Mr. Morricone's business slowed down. On these cold winter days we sometimes found ourselves alone in the parlor as Mr. Morricone whisked and whipped and prepared our orders. He was a large man who took his work seriously. Standing there, alone with the man and his ice cream, it sometimes occurred to us that there was something a little sinister about the blood-red sauce that dripped down the side of the Drive-By Double Cone. Or we would watch the chocolate chunks slowly sinking down the center of the Lead Boot Lemon Lush and wonder whether Mr. Morricone had always been an ice cream man. Some of us would notice that the miniature flakes in the Mowed Down Madness looked just like bodies collapsing to the ground.

On quiet days like this, Mr. Morricone would sometimes invite us to stay and eat our ice creams in the shop. We felt nervous about this, but it was cold outside and it felt rude to say no, so we would sit down in one of the booths and listen to Mr. Morricone's stories about Larkin Mills in the good old days.

The good old days, according to Mr. Morricone, were those when crime was an organized, civilized affair, unlike the ramshackle business it had become. Back then, he would say, ordinary folk could walk down any street in any part of the town without fear, because no one did anything criminal without the say so of The Roof.

He had lots of stories about the good old days but our favorite was the one about the location of the shop. We knew the story was true because we had heard others tell it, but no one told it as well as Mr. Morricone.

It went something like this.

No one knew where The Roof came from, or how he rose so high in the world of organized crime, but at the height of his powers there wasn't a single business in Larkin Mills that The Roof didn't have a stake in. Nothing was too big or too small. He controlled everyone from the mayor right down to the men who collected the bins.

No one knew The Roof's real name. Or if they did they kept quiet about it. Mr. Morricone would explain that The Roof's real name was unimportant. He was a symbol. He looked after everyone's interests. He protected them all. He kept them safe. People believed in him. Journalists foolish enough to go digging into his true identity would either get paid off, or weighed down and dropped into the Larkin Mills reservoir along with all of The Roof's enemies. At one point, the reservoir became so polluted with bodies, the town's water supply ran red. As with all problems in Larkin Mills during this golden age, this one was solved quickly and efficiently. The reservoir was emptied and cleaned and an experimental tidal-based sewage system was installed to flush out the system. After that The Roof found new places to hide his victims' bodies, such as plastering them behind the walls in one of the many new developments he had built. To this day, Mr. Morricone would tell us, the town was full of unseen corpses. Sometimes they would start to smell and the buildings would have to be de-corpsed.

In spite of the mystery surrounding his name, The Roof was by no means an invisible presence in Larkin Mills. During his public appearances, he was always seen wearing his bowler hat and tailor-made suit, and holding an enormous cigar between his teeth. Restaurant owners would have their photos taken with him, then put the framed pictures up on their walls. An oil portrait of the man hung in the atrium of the Larkin Mills National Museum. There was even a life-sized wax model of him in Madam Letrec's World of Wax. The plaque in front of the model explained that The Roof had kindly donated his hat, cigar and gun to the exhibit. The model was cast with one hand tucked in his waistcoat pocket and the other pointing the gun, finger on the trigger. Visitors to the museum would often pose with the barrel to their heads, as though The Roof was about to shoot them, then hide their dead bodies.

"These were simpler, happier times," Mr. Morricone would tell us, while finely slicing a chocolate-dipped strawberry. He would pause and point the knife at us. "But every Caesar has some ambitious young Brutus waiting in the wings with a dagger in hand and designs on the empire."

In this case, it was a man named Frank Finchley. He held various roles, such as The Roof's personal plasterer and the mayor's chauffeur, before setting his sights on a higher position. Strange rumors surrounded him. Some said he had the power to hypnotize people with the touch of his hand. Some said that he kept a wild puma as a pet. Our favorite story was the one about the peak of his black cap being made from the horn of a rhinoceros he killed with his bare hands. Whatever the truth, no one ever dared ask the man about these stories. Finchley was as ruthless as he was ambitious. Growing tired of taking The Roof's orders, he decided to go it alone. He was by no means the first challenger, but The Roof seemed strangely reluctant to cut down this burgeoning problem before it grew too big. Some people said that the two men looked similar and a few even believed that Finchley was The Roof's son, but no one knew for sure, especially as The Roof had a habit of referring to all his employees as his children.

Finchley was gifted in the subtle art of persuasion. When he convinced The Roof's four most trusted employees to switch allegiances, his old employer had no choice but to agree to meet with him to resolve the situation. A number of possible locations for the meeting were rejected until, eventually, both parties agreed on a brand new development recently built in a quiet part of town. The Roof's people searched it thoroughly for hidden explosives or false walls. They found nothing. Snipers were placed on the building across the road and, when The Roof arrived, he brought a six-man security team. He must have known that there was a high chance that he was walking into a trap. He was right. As soon as he entered, the whole place went up in flames. There were no survivors.

Mr. Morricone explained that Finchley had plastered the place himself some years before and had placed explosives inside the walls.

The Roof's reign was over.

Finchley seized control of the town but quickly discovered how vital The Roof had been to its smooth running. Where The Roof had inspired loyalty, Finchley received treachery. People worshipped The Roof. They feared Finchley. He trusted no one and nobody trusted him. He was every bit as ruthless but never so kind. There was no way he could keep a firm grip on such a large territory. The town's crime became fractured and divided. More rivals sprang up, some loyal to the memory of the The Roof, others who had been waiting for someone else to get him out of the way. Gang warfare ruled. The streets were no longer safe for anyone.

"Finchley had brought chaos to Larkin Mills but, such was the man's arrogance that he refused to accept it was his fault," Mr. Morricone would tell us while pounding a bag of almonds with the thick end of a rolling pin.

Instead, Finchley blamed his predecessor's legacy. He believed that the town was still in the shadow of its previous crime lord and that it would not be able to progress until it stepped out from that shadow. Finchley pledged to remove every memory of the man. The signed pictures on the café walls were destroyed. Sometimes the cafés were burned down. The portrait in the museum was removed. Anyone who spoke publicly in praise of The Roof either lived to regret it or wound up in an early grave.

The last thing remaining was the waxwork. One grey Sunday morning, Finchley arrived outside Madam Letrec's World of Wax with a van full of armed goons.

The museum was not famous for the accuracy of its waxworks but The Roof's model was disturbingly realistic. Standing in front of it was like being in the same room as the man himself. Maybe this was why Finchley told his men to stand outside. He needed a moment alone with it.

At this stage in the story, Mr. Morricone would point out that this was before the days of CCTV cameras so no one knew for sure what happened in that room. Those standing outside

66

the room said they heard shouting and arguing. They assumed Finchley was letting off steam at his old boss.

Then there was a gunshot.

And another.

Six shots were fired in total, and when Finchley's men shouldered the door open they discovered they needed a new boss. Finchley was dead. He had been shot six times. The gun that had shot him was in the hand of the waxwork model and was still smoking. In fear or anger, one of the goons fired three shots at the waxwork model. Each one went straight through the wax.

Following Finchley's death, the police and authorities were able to regain greater control over the town. The gangs were running scared. Crime became disorganized, unpredictable and sporadic.

Mayor Kendall brought in new laws to help the police arrest crime lords. An investigation was launched into Finchley's death. The forensic evidence confirmed that Finchley was killed by a gun held by the waxwork model. The only finger-prints on the gun were The Roof's, which was no surprise since it had belonged to him. It was concluded that it had been loaded this whole time. All those visitors had stood in front of a loaded gun. An expert testified that it was possible for a wax-work to move. He listed temperature and other environmental conditions amongst the reasons that the trigger finger might have contracted. He conceded that it was an extreme coinci-dence that it would squeeze the gun trigger six times and kill The Roof's murderer. As unlikely as this explanation was, it was the only one available to the judge so he reached the ver-dict of Accidental Death by Irony.

The waxwork model of The Roof was melted down and

remolded into a model of the councillor who passed the law to have it melted down. Finchley had succeeded in removing from the town the last image of The Roof.

Some of us believed that The Roof faked his death. Perhaps he switched places with the waxwork, pulled the trigger, then got out through one of the secret passageways we had heard about in the museum walls. Maybe he had arranged the whole thing. Maybe he had always maintained a distinctive appearance so that he could adopt a new look when he wanted to retire. After all, who would recognize the man three decades later without his hat, suit, cigar and gun?

Mr. Morricone had no time for this kind of speculation. As far as he was concerned The Roof died in the shop that was to become the ice cream parlor. Mr. Morricone chose colorful names for his creations in homage to the man who had died there. When we told him our conspiracy theories, Mr. Morricone would shake his head and say, "What? You think a man that powerful could give it all up and lead a normal life? What would he do, this man? Perhaps he would set up an ice cream parlor and spend the rest of his days selling hundreds and thousands to children?" Mr. Morricone would laugh. "The very idea. No, sorry. The Roof is dead. It's just that sometimes even the dead get revenge."

He would then suggest we try one of his latest creations, which would be called something like Honeycomb Agony or Trigger Finger of Fudge or Vanilla Vengeance.

Egg of the Dead

1.

THE UNUSUALLY HIGH LEVELS of nitrogen in the soil and pockets of concentrated oxygen under Larkin Mills meant that any archaeological digs in the area had some of the highest mortality rates in the country. The smallest spark could cause an explosion of atomic proportions, but for George Parson, it was worth the risk.

"Hand us the nylon 3 B, would you, Park?" Mr. Parson lay on his stomach with one hand reaching behind him.

His daughter, whose name was Seraphina but called herself Park, looked at the large box of brushes, neatly arranged in order of size and material. She ran her finger across the bottom and checked three times that she had the right one.

"Come on, Park," said Mr. Parson.

She checked one more time, then handed him the brush.

"It's getting dark." Park had no interest in archaeology but, since her father refused to waste money on a qualified assistant, it was down to her to keep him alive.

"The bottle moths provide ample lighting," said Mr. Parson. Park looked up at the blue glow of the buzzing insects in the trees.

"Did you know bottle moths are completely unique to Larkin Mills?" said Mr. Parson. "It is said they first glowed following the great storm of 47 AD. Back then, this was still an unnamed settlement being used as a base for the invading armies of Commander Clodius Albinus."

"You've told me all this before." Park was worried her father wasn't concentrating on what he was doing.

"So, can you tell me what the philosopher Boethius wrote about the storm?"

"He believed it was caused by some kind of alien landing," said Park. "I think you need the duck-feather brush for this bit."

"Good girl. You'll make a first-rate archaeologist one day, just like your mother."

Park handed him the brush. When Larkin Mills Council had rejected her parents' outlandish theory and refused to give them a grant for this dig, Mr. and Mrs. Parson had packed up their things and took on a series of jobs to raise the money themselves. The more dangerous the dig, the better the pay. Park's mother had died using a copper brush in an unstable Patagonian dig where speed had been prioritized over safety.

"I have school tomorrow," said Park.

"Can't you skip it?"

"It's my first day, Dad. New town, new school. Again. Remember? We haven't even checked into our hotel yet. I need a shower. I need some sleep."

"But Park, this dig . . . "

"Dad, I know how important this dig is to you, but it's my first day at my fifth school this year."

"Yes, but this is Larkin Mills. Finally I'll be able to make my name. This is where we can make sure that your mother didn't die in vain."

"By digging up some old broken pots."

Park could tell by his silence she had annoyed him.

"I just need some sleep. In an actual bed. We both do," she pleaded.

Mr. Parson rolled over and looked at his watch. "All right, I'll tell you what. Why don't you grab a couple of hours' sleep in the tent and, when I'm done with this layer, we'll both go to the hotel."

"Other children aren't forced to sleep in tents before their first day of school."

"Then other children's parents are obviously not on the brink of the most exciting discovery in the history of archaeology."

Park knew there was no point arguing so went to unravel her sleeping bag. She didn't like leaving her father, but she was tired and too likely to make a mistake herself. Given the choice, she would rather her father's death was his own fault than hers, but she did wonder what kind of parent forced his child to make such a choice in the first place.

It was cold inside the tent and the ground was rock hard but Park was exhausted and soon fell asleep. When she awoke it was lighter and her father was leaning over her.

"Park," he said. "Get up. Come and see. You have to see this."

"Is it a broken pot?" she asked.

"No, come and look."

Park unzipped the sleeping bag and followed him out of the tent. The sky was a pale blue. In the ground was a large grey oval object covered in dirt.

"It looks like a big egg," said Park.

"Isn't it intriguing?" replied Mr. Parson.

"Probably less so to the bird that laid it."

"A bird's egg would have decomposed." He tapped it with the end of his trowel. "Boethius wrote about an egg. He called it the *Ovum Vitae* ... The Egg of Life."

"Is it something to do with the aliens?"

Her father nodded.

"So what does it do, this egg?"

"Some believe that to touch it brings instant death. Others, that it has the power to reawaken the dead. Boethius said it contained the secrets of the universe."

"You will be careful, won't you?" Park said nervously.

Mr. Parson smiled. "Park, what happened to your mother was a terrible accident but I promise you, I'm here for the long run."

"But you won't touch it, will you?"

"You need to trust that I know what I'm doing."

"Mum knew what she was doing."

Her father sighed.

"You look tired." Park noticed the dark bags under her dad's eyes. "Promise me you'll get some sleep before any more digging."

He kissed the top of her head. "Very sensible. Just like your mother. I'll get my sleeping bag."

"No. Not in the tent. You need to get some proper rest."

"All right. I'll book us into the hotel."

"I'll meet you there after school."

"School?"

"It's my first day and the sun is coming up. I'd better get ready. Will you come and collect me at the end of the day?"

"Yes, yes, of course," said Mr. Parson, gazing at the egg.

2.

Park's first day at school was strikingly similar to all her other first days. The teacher misinterpreted her lack of interest as shyness and allocated a pupil to act as her buddy for the day. The boy's name was Campbell Milkwell. He had pale skin and empty eyes. Unlike the other pupils who wore ties in accordance with the current fashion (the knot to one side) his was tied extremely neatly. He looked neither pleased nor annoyed to be given the task of looking after the new girl.

"Did you get thrown out of your last school?" he asked as they walked to the science block for their first lesson.

"No. My dad moves around a lot. He's an archaeologist."

"Mine runs the funeral guest house."

"What's a funeral guest house?" asked Park.

"Part funeral parlor, part hotel."

"Are there dead people in the hotel?" Park was mildly appalled by the idea.

"Yes. They don't use the room service as much as the living guests. That's one of my dad's jokes. It's not funny, I know. I don't know why I say it. Habit, I suppose."

"Isn't it creepy having all those dead bodies around?"

"You get used to it," he said. "This is our classroom."

The first day passed as first days always did: boringly. Her father may have considered Larkin Mills to be the most interesting place in the world, but it was pretty ordinary as far as

Park was concerned. At the end of the day, Park stood at the gate with Campbell.

"My dad's booked us into a hotel," she said. "Only it looks like he's forgotten to pick me up."

"I'll show you the way if you like. We can walk together."

"But you don't know which hotel. Come to think of it, nor do I."

"There's only one hotel in Larkin Mills," said Campbell casually.

"Yours?" It was typical, thought Park, that the one time her dad agreed to book them into a hotel, it was one with a bunch of dead bodies. "It's a big town to only have one hotel."

"There used to be more," said Campbell. "The Larkin Grand was shut down after a toad infestation. The Cosmopolitan turned out to be built on a locust nest. The Metropolitan was flooded by the abattoir next door. There were others but they all went under: lice, disease, death of the firstborn. Anyway, now it's just us. I think we should rename it Dead and Breakfast, but Dad doesn't approve of using the D-word. Come on, then." Campbell threw his bag over his shoulder and they set off. "There's a big game on tonight and I don't want to miss the build up."

"Football?" Park had precisely zero interest in sport.

"Competitive basket weaving," said Campbell.

"Is that a game?"

"You've never heard of competitive basket weaving?" said Campbell. "It's huge here. There are two teams, the Larkin Lions and the Mad Millers. The Millers are my team, except they recently sold all their players and bought all of the Lions' players, so I'm thinking about switching."

Park wondered if there was any chance this was a joke but

it didn't appear to be.

"What does it involve?"

"Weaving baskets, of course. Albino Rodriquez is our best player. Except he's now weaving for the Lions. He can weave a medium-sized trug in under five minutes."

"Right."

Campbell talked about basket weaving all the way to the hotel, which turned out to be an imposing red-brick building with gargoyles adorning the roof and the date 1835 carved into the top.

"It looks properly old, doesn't it?" said Campbell. "You'd hardly believe it was built less than forty years ago."

"What about the date?"

"Six thirty-five was the time it was finished. Anyway, home sweet funeral home," said Campbell. "Let's get you checked in."

Campbell held the door open for her. The reception was decorated in velvet and gold. To the right of the door was a sad-looking stone angel with her palms held out. Opposite this was a table with leaflets advertising types of casket, funeral photographers and Madam Letrec's World of Wax. Serene classical music played from discreet speakers.

Campbell walked over to the empty reception desk and opened a large book. He ran his finger down the page. "You and your dad have adjoining rooms on the fourth floor." He took a key from a hook behind him. "Here."

Park felt the coldness of his fingers on her palm as he handed her the key.

"Thanks," she said. "Don't you have any staff?"

"Of course," said Campbell, "but Dad has an event this afternoon. It must have overrun."

"An event?"

75

"That's what we're supposed to call funerals when we're around the hotel. There's a television in your room but you can come and watch the match in the communal room if you want. It starts at eight but I'll be down there from six for the build up."

"Okay." Park pressed the button to call the lift.

"You'll need to hit number three to get to the fourth floor because of the subsidence," said Campbell.

"What does that mean?"

"The building's sinking. This used to be the first floor. The old ground floor is in the cellar now. Dad reckons that by the time I'm his age, the second floor will be the first floor and then you'll need to press two to get to the fourth floor."

"The building is sinking?" Park looked uncertainly at the rickety lift.

"Yes, something to do with being built on marshland. It's sinking but at different rates."

"Is it safe?"

"I think so. Dad says everything is sinking. It's just that we're sinking a little faster. Back when he bought it, it had two more floors but they're down in the cellar now."

"It seems like a big building for a funeral parlor."

"Dad says that back in the good old days, funerals were big business. People were dropping like flies back then. Sounds a bit sinister, I know, but that's parents for you. One day, I'll take over the business. Dad says the funeral business is good because, rich or poor, you can't stop people dying."

Park stepped into the lift and Campbell slid the metal grate shut behind her. "I'll see you later, then," he said hopefully.

Park smiled and pressed the button. The lift juddered its way up to the fourth floor. When she stepped out of the lift she found an old lady there, looking decidedly lost.

"Excuse me, dear, I wonder if you could help me." She wore a pale blue twin-set and blouse. Her arms were as thing as twigs and she used a stick to walk. "I'm trying to find a cup of tea. I'm absolutely parched."

"Have you tried room service?"

"I can't find a telephone."

"Isn't there a kettle in the room?" asked Park, who had stayed in a lot of hotels.

"I've looked everywhere but I can't find one," said the old lady. She leaned in and spoke softly. "Between you and me, this feels more like a morgue than a hotel."

"I'll see if there's a kettle in my room," said Park. She found her door number and, after wrestling with the key, stepped inside. It looked like every other hotel room she had stayed in. There was a small square television, two thin white towels in the bathroom, and a tray on the dresser with a small kettle and drink sachets in a cup.

"Why don't you come in and sit down?" said Park. "I'll make you a cup of tea."

"That's very kind of you, dear," said the old lady. As she lowered herself into a wicker chair, Park wondered whether the cracking noise was coming from the chair or the woman's bones.

"I'm Dorothy. Everyone calls me Dot but, if I'm honest, I rather wish they wouldn't. It just sounds so small and unimportant, doesn't it? A dot. I've never liked it."

Park filled the kettle with water from the bathroom tap and switched it on. "Do you take sugar?" she asked when it was boiling.

"Not usually but I think I will today. I'm awfully shaky."

77

Park stirred the teabag, added the milk and sugar, then passed it to Dorothy. "Careful. It's hot."

The old woman gripped the cup, then threw the contents down her throat in one go. She handed her the cup back. "Thank you. You're a very kind young lady." She tried to stand up but wouldn't have managed it without Park's help. Her wrinkled arm felt as cold as ice.

"Would you like me to help you find your room?" offered Park.

"No. You've been quite kind enough for one day. I shan't have you thinking of me as a charity case. Good night."

"Good night, Dorothy."

Park closed the door and went to turn on the television. There was a show on in which two competitors were racing to wallpaper their houses, with increasingly challenging obstacles such as damp walls, inferior wallpaper paste and untamed lions being released into the rooms. Park switched off the television when she heard a door open. Her father stood in the doorway between the two rooms. His hair was messy and his face was creased from sleep. He wore a baggy pair of tartan pajamas.

"Hello, darling." He yawned. "How was school?"

"Like school. You look terrible."

"I do feel a little fuzzy around the edges, now you mention it. Come and see the egg. It's everything we hoped . . . and more."

"You are being careful, aren't you?" said Park.

"Don't worry. I keep telling you. I know what I'm doing. Come see."

She followed him into his bathroom. There was a line of muddy residue around the top of the bath. The egg was in the sink. Two rubber gloves were draped over the side. The dirt had been washed off to reveal a perfectly smooth grey surface. There were no ancient markings or mysterious hieroglyphics. To Park, it looked as ordinary and dull as one of her father's broken pots.

"What's it made of?" she asked.

"It isn't a material that naturally occurs on this planet," he said, his eyes wide with awe and wonder.

"So it's a meteorite?" said Park, plainly.

"It is Boethius' egg. It's the Egg of Life, only it isn't what we what we thought."

"But you just said—"

"I know, I know. It's so much more than we could have imagined. Look, I've been writing." She followed him back into the bedroom and saw a huge wad of paper filled with frantic scrawl. She picked up the top piece and read the title aloud. *The Soothsayer and the Dwarf.* Is it a story?"

She turned around to find her father drinking from a plastic cup. "I'm sorry," he said. "I've had such a dry throat since the dig. Must be all that dust. Yes, it's a story."

"Why are you writing a story?"

"Because there's so much I now understand. I'm trying to make sense of it all, but I must be careful. It isn't just the council who will object this time. Every major religion will be on my back, not to mention the atheists ... No one will accept my findings readily, but it's true. I swear, it's all true."

"About the alien?"

"Aliens," said her father. "Two beings – a master and his rebellious servant. Two forces locked in an eternal conflict that they brought here to Earth. A struggle that has been misunderstood and misrepresented throughout history."

"You're not making any sense, Dad."

79

"God and the devil, Park," he said, breathing heavily. "Right here in Larkin Mills."

"What?"

"I'm sorry, Park. I have to work. After another drink." He bent down and drank straight from the tap.

3.

Park had planned to go downstairs to watch the television with Campbell but it had been a long time since she had felt the comfort of a real bed and, as soon as she lay down, she fell asleep. When she awoke, her father was gone and so was the egg. He had left a note on her bathroom mirror that read: *Morning, Park. Gone to library. Love, Dad.*

Park dressed and went downstairs for breakfast, which turned out to be a lackluster buffet consisting of two large plastic containers filled with cereal, half a bottle of milk, a jug of orange juice with something floating in it, a bowl of dry dates and a loaf of unsliced bread beside an ancient toaster. Park poured herself a bowl of cornflakes and sat down to eat.

"Morning." Campbell came out of the kitchen. "You missed an amazing game last night. It went to penalty stitching. The Millers got through on the last one. I think I'm going back to supporting them. It was brilliant."

"Sorry. I fell asleep," she replied.

"It's the semi-finals tonight. You should definitely watch that. You haven't lived until you've sat through all three hours of a competitive basket weaving semi-final."

"Three hours?"

"Unless it goes into extra time, of course."

Park looked around the room. "It's very quiet in here."

"You and your dad are the only guests at the moment."

"What about the old lady I met last night?"

"What old lady?"

"She couldn't find a kettle in her room."

Campbell shrugged. "Probably one of the street wanderers. They get in sometimes and make themselves at home. I'll tell Dad to do a sweep of your floor."

"She was very old and confused."

"Didn't know where she was? Couldn't find her room?" asked Campbell.

"Exactly like that."

"Oh, she's probably from the Residential Home for the Extremely Inactive. That lot are always finding their way in and getting confused."

"How do they get in?"

"Because every time Dad makes the place secure another part of the building sinks and opens up a new way in. Don't worry. Dad will get her back to where she needs to be."

On Park's second day at the school, she identified all the usual cliques, clans and gangs. She spent most of the day with Campbell, who was just about the only one who was different. She liked that about him. He was refreshingly invisible. He was not bullied or teased. He was accepted, ignored and allowed to drift through the school like a ghost. She liked how some of that ghost-like quality rubbed off on her, although this wasn't the case with his enthusiasm for professional basket weaving. That evening, he talked about it all the way back to the hotel, where they found a long black car parked outside the front.

"It must be one of the late guests checking out," said Campbell.

"You mean one of the dead ones?"

"Remember the rule about the D-word. Dad says there are over five hundred ways of talking about the dead, and that undertakers should favor softer words."

"You're not an undertaker, though, are you?"

"I will be one day, just like my father and his father. Apparently my great grandfather was a pall-bearer for Queen Victoria."

Park could see the coffin through the hearse's spotless windows. Around it were three wreaths of flowers, spelling out the words, *MUM, NAN* and *DOT*.

"Dot?" said Park.

"Apparently she'd asked for Dorothy but the family didn't want to pay for that," Campbell told her. "You get charged by the letter."

"Dot? But ... when did she die?"

"About a week ago."

"What?"

Campbell looked at her. "If you're going to get this upset every time there's a funeral, you've picked the wrong hotel to stay at. Not that you had any choice."

Park peered into the hearse at the photograph of the old lady she had met the previous evening. "She was sitting in my room last night. I made her a cup of tea."

Campbell smiled. "Dad says we should treat our late guests with equal respect to our paying guests but we don't normally offer them room service. I'm making popcorn for the big game. I'll make a whole bucket and we can share if you like."

Park wondered if Campbell believed her. She wasn't sure if she believed herself. When she got back to her room, she found the unwashed teacup still on the sideboard next to the empty sugar sachet. Her father was still out, so she switched on the television to the same show, only now the audience were deciding whose house should be hit with the demolition ball. The contestants were desperately begging to be spared, which the audience found hilarious. Park watched the show for slightly longer than she could bear, then took the lift down to the communal room.

"You're just in time," said Campbell. "The highlights from the last game are on."

Competitive basket weaving was even duller than Park had expected. Not that you would have believed it to hear the commentators, excitedly describing every detail. Occasionally Campbell would ask whether she wanted anything explained.

"I think I'm following it now," she lied, fearful of lengthy explanations.

By the end of the three-hour game, the Larkin Lions had five baskets to Mad Millers' eight, but taking into account the quality of the baskets, the panel of adjudicators had given the match to the Lions, much to the crowd's delight and to Campbell's annoyance. He was talking about switching allegiances again when Park said good night. She went out into the lobby and pressed the lift button. The door slid open to reveal a woman inside. "Well?" she said. "Getting in or not?" From her appearance and aroma, Park took her to be one of the vagrants Campbell mentioned.

"I'll take the stairs," said Park.

"Suit yourself," replied the woman.

It was the first time she had walked up the stairs so it was confusing to find that it only took two flights to reach her floor. When she finally got back to her room she was relieved to see that her father had returned. She eased open the door and looked in to see him fast asleep in the bed with the bathroom light on.

4.

Since her mother's death, Park had been dreading the day archaeology took her father's life. The next morning, she lay in bed, feeling comforted by his snores. She was pleased he was sleeping well. Soon, he could present his egg to the Royal Society of Archaeology. They would have to give him the credit he craved, then there would be no more digging. No more fear.

Stepping into the lift, she was hit by the smell, presumably left by the vagrant she had met the previous night. She wondered how it was possible for anyone to live with such a stench.

She planned to tell Campbell about it but, when she reached the breakfast hall, she saw that it was full of vagrants. Most were old, but not all. The woman from the lift had Campbell backed into a corner, while she complained loudly.

"Where's my prunes?" yelled a vile woman. "I always have prunes for breakfast. Every morning, otherwise I have all kinds of problems."

"I'm sorry," said Campbell. "I'll see if I can find a tin."

"It's not good enough, young man. I need my prunes. Also, what's wrong with the heating in this place? My room is like an ice bucket. I need to speak to my son. I need to speak to Albert."

Campbell apologized again then extracted himself from the conversation to join Park.

"Where did they all come from?" she asked.

Campbell's eyes revealed undisguised horror. "They're late guests," he whispered. "They're late guests!"

"What?"

"They're dead. All of them."

"Dead?"

"Mrs. Dance – the one asking for prunes – she's been on ice all week, while her brother flies over from Australia for the funeral."

"So the smell . . . " began Park.

"Decomposing bodies," hissed Campbell. "It doesn't make any sense. All these dead people have woken up . . . and they want breakfast."

"Woken up?" Park remembered her father's words about the egg. *It has the power to reawaken the dead.* "Of course," she said. "It really can bring the dead back."

"What can?"

"The egg."

"Eggs? I just told Mr. Riley. We're all out."

"Stay here." Park ran out of the dining hall, up the stairs. She went into her room, then through the adjoining door into her father's. He was sitting on his bed, watching the television show in which the finalists were being nailed to a piece of wood, while the audience clapped and laughed.

"What's wrong?" he said. "You look worried."

"I need to borrow it. The egg."

"Why? What is it?"

"I just need to see something." She darted into the bathroom, wrapped the egg in a towel and picked it up.

"Park, don't. Please."

"I'll be back in a minute."

She ran out onto the landing and pressed the lift button. When it arrived, there was a man standing inside. He wore a smart suit with a blue flower in his lapel. His face was deathly white and his eyes were dark grey. Park was about to make her excuses, when he spotted the large bundle she was clutching.

"What have you there, then?"

"Er . . . washing?" she replied.

"We have a service to clean it for you. Leave it in your room and my son will pick it up."

"You're Mr. Milkwell."

"I am. Are you going down?"

"Yes."

"Whereas I am going up." He stepped out of the lift.

"I'll take the stairs."

"No, I insist." Mr. Milkwell held the door open. "You are a paying guest. You take priority. Mrs. Dance won't mind waiting."

"I think you'd be surprised."

"I'm sorry?" Mr. Milkwell raised a quizzical eyebrow.

"Nothing." Park stepped into the lift. "Thank you. Have a good day."

"The same to you." The doors slid shut and Park took the lift to ground level, where she found Campbell being hassled by a bunch of corpses about the strength of the tea in the urn.

"He'll make a fresh one in a minute," said Park, dragging Campbell to one side. "Take this." She handed him the egg. "Take it out of the hotel."

"What?"

"Carry it out."

"Why?"

"I need to see something."

"How far?"

"I don't know. Take it across the road."

"You want me to take this big egg for a walk?"

"Yes, but don't touch it. I'll explain later. Just go."

"All right."

Park watched out of a window as Campbell crossed the road with the egg. He turned back to look at her. She looked over her shoulder at the breakfasting corpses. She waved Campbell on. He continued walking away. He had reached the orphanage when Park heard thuds and clattering cutlery. She turned around to see that all of the corpses were lying still. Dead again. A half-eaten pear rolled along the dining room floor.

"It works," she whispered. "The egg brings back the dead."

She had to tell her father. She took the stairs two at a time to the fourth floor and burst into the room. "Dad! Dad," she yelled. "It works! It actually works! The egg really does reawaken the dead."

There was no response. She pushed open the door to find her father lying in his bed. Unmoving. He wasn't snoring. Nor breathing. Mr. Parson was dead.

Park dropped to his side. She took his cold right hand in hers and wept into his pajama sleeves.

Five minutes later, Campbell grew bored of standing around with a big egg and returned to the hotel. As he walked back into the building, Park's father opened his eyes, yawned, stretched and got up to fetch a drink. Noticing his daughter crying, he asked what was wrong.

"You promised me you wouldn't touch it," she said.

"I'm sorry," said Mr. Parson. "I had to understand how it worked."

"You knew! You knew it would kill you and you still did it."

"I'm still here as long as we have the egg," Park's father told her. "Park, you have to understand. This egg. One touch shows you the lives of everything that has ever died."

"Including you."

Mr. Parson downed his cup of water then instantly refilled it. "I needed to know the truth."

"And I needed a father."

"Park, this kind of discovery is much bigger than us. It's everything your mother and I were searching for. It's all that matters to me."

"Yes, I understand that now." Park sat down next to her father to watch the end of the television show, in which the last remaining contestant was trying to avoid being torn apart by four wild horses, while the audience argued over which horse should be whipped first.

"What an idiot," said Mr. Parson. "I knew he should have gone for the ice cream."

The Soothsayer and the Dwarf

By George Parson

1.

WE KNOW from the writings of Boethius the philosopher that Larkin the soothsayer appeared on the night of the great storm of 47 AD. The Roman invaders had grown accustomed to Britain's unsavory weather but this storm was unlike anything previously experienced. Boethius wrote of strange colors filling the sky. Great lumps of ice fell, even though it was a warm summer night. He also noted that throughout the storm, the stars remained unhidden by clouds.

The Roman priests warned that it was the judgment of Jupiter, angry at the blood spilled to conquer the people of this foreign island. The defeated Celts believed it was Taranis, their god of Thunder, wreaking revenge on these vile intruders. Boethius was a famous atheist so had a more scientific interest in the strange phenomenon. He picked up a lantern and made his way to the base of a nearby hill where he observed a strange blue glow high in the trees. He climbed to the top of the hill and found a stranger standing in a clearing there. The tall man was stark naked, with fresh burn marks all over his skin.

"It is very cold to be without one's robes," said Boethius.

"That's funny," replied the man. "It feels devilishly warm down here to me."

"How did you come to be standing here on such a night without robes?" asked Boethius.

"It is a long story. Let us say that I fell here," said the man, rubbing the two small bumps at his temples.

Boethius looked up at the trees. If the man had fallen from one of those, he would have surely been covered in scratches and scrapes, rather than the burns that covered his body.

"Where am I?" asked the man.

"I do not know the name of this spot," said Boethius. "I imagine that the Britons have a name for it but I am unaware of it."

"What is a Briton?"

"A local to these parts."

"Are you not local?"

"No. I am a Roman. I must say, yours is a very strange manner."

"As is yours to me," replied the stranger.

"I came here in search of the object that fell from the sky," said Boethius.

"Clothe me, feed me and teach me the customs of this land, and I will reveal all you desire to know."

"Are you a beggar that you would ask so much?"

"No," said the man, suddenly sounding very angry. "I am no beggar. No longer. I offer an exchange of knowledge. Tell me what I want to know and I will deliver to you the secrets of the universe."

"It is a bold claim for a man with no clothes."

"I have no clothes, but I do have one possession. Wait one moment. I will show you." The man disappeared into the bushes. Boethius did not follow him but, in the shadows, caught a glimpse of a pair of ram's horns. He did not see the beast to whom they belonged and soon the stranger returned, carrying a large oval object wrapped in leaves.

"What is it?" asked Boethius.

"It is called the Egg of Life."

Boethius reached out a hand out to touch the egg, but the man stepped back.

"Do not touch it directly. The egg contains great knowledge but also much danger to a mortal hand."

"You seem unconcerned for one holding such a dangerous object," reasoned Boethius.

"I am not the same as you."

Boethius wondered if this was a man to fear after all, but if the stranger was dangerous, he was also undeniably intriguing. "What is your name?" he asked.

"I think here I shall be called Larkin," replied the man.

"Then come, Larkin, let us find you some robes," said Boethius.

He took the stranger to his house on the outskirts of town, which he shared with his slave, whom he had named Candle, because of how his Celtic name sounded to him. Despite the language barrier and obvious intellectual inferiority, Boethius discovered that Candle was capable of following orders when they were spoken loudly and clearly.

"Candle, make bed . . . Make food and bring wine. We have a

guest. Oh, and bring robes."

The slave nodded and left. Larkin placed the egg on a plinth in the center of the dining room. When Candle returned with food, drink and clothes, Larkin and Boethius sat down to eat.

"Your home is very dark," said Larkin.

"I can have my slave light more lamps if you desire," replied Boethius.

"I did not mean your dwelling. I meant this place you call home." He gesticulated out of the window.

"But ... but it is night," said Boethius.

"What does that mean?"

"You have never heard of night, when the world is devoid of light?"

"Sadly not," said Larkin. "Light is always present in my homeland. What is the cause of such darkness?"

"It occurs when the sun is on the other side of the world."

"This sun sounds powerful. I would speak with him."

"The sun is a burning orb a great distance from here. I do not think I can get you an audience with it."

The man nodded. "So who *is* in charge of this world?"

"That would be Emperor Commodus. He rules our empire from his home in Rome. Sadly, I fear an audience with him would be no easier to obtain."

"Where I am from, the powerful often distribute responsibility to others."

"It is the same here," said Boethius. "Clodius Albinus, the youngest of the emperor's brothers, rules the armies on this island. You must have travelled from a long way to be unaware of the greatest empire the world has ever known."

"A great distance indeed," agreed Larkin.

"Then how have you ended up in this drizzly little corner of the world?"

"You think this place insignificant?"

"Yes. It is devoid of culture." Candle refilled Boethius' cup of wine. "Thank you. And it is populated by thick-browed barbarians."

Larkin glanced at Candle, then back to his host. "Then why are you here?"

"I spoke out against a powerful institution, meaning I was cast out of the city of my birth."

Larkin smiled and placed a hand on Boethius' shoulder. "My friend," he said. "I believe you and I have much in common, but perhaps we can talk more when your sun has returned. I am tired from my journey and must get some rest."

"Of course," said Boethius. "Candle, show our guest to bed."

Candle nodded and led Larkin out. Boethius stood and examined the egg. It rested on the plinth and the foliage that had surrounded it had fallen away, revealing its grey exterior. Boethius was aware of some materials that were poisonous or harmful to the touch but this one looked as dull and harmless as slate. He reached out his hands and placed his palms on either side of it.

At first it felt cold to the touch but slowly it warmed until it was scolding hot. He tried to move his hands away but was unable. The pain spread from his fingertips, through his body. He saw in a single instant the death of everything. From single-cell organisms to the largest life forms; he witnessed all of life die. He saw visions of the dragons roaming the earth before man. He understood that mankind was a mere intake of breath compared with all that had gone before it. In the grand scheme of the universe, it was a single heartbeat of an ant. His mouth went cold and he felt sweetness on his tongue before a great unquenchable thirst consumed him. He dropped to his knees and drank a goblet of wine, but his thirst remained. He released the empty vessel, pressed his hands together and, for the first time in many years, prayed to God.

2.

The following morning, Larkin found Candle in the kitchen, chopping some kind of vegetable with a knife as long as his forearm.

"Where is your master?" asked Larkin.

"You speak my language?" replied the slave, who was accustomed to being addressed in Latin.

"I speak many languages," said Larkin. "Now, where is Boethius? Is he still asleep?"

"He has not slept all night."

"Why? Does he fear you will murder him in his bed?"

"I should kill you for saying such a thing." Candle pointed the tip of the knife at Larkin.

"You should kill yourself for not already having done so. They slay your men and shame your women, and you pour their wine and change their sheets."

Candle looked away in shame. "I lost my honor when I was defeated on the battlefield."

Larkin smiled. "After dining on the bitterness of defeat, one needs something as sweet as vengeance for a dessert."

Candle felt the soft caress of Larkin's subtly persuasive words. "What do you want?"

"I want to know what Boethius is doing if not sleeping."

"He writes."

"Why?"

"The only reason men like him write – to be remembered."

"What use is fame to the dead? If you want something you must grab it in this life." Larkin placed a hand on Candle's shoulder and stared intently into his eyes. "Vengeance."

"Vengeance," repeated Candle. He ran a finger along the edge of his knife, drawing a line of blood. "Your words are my instruction. I will slit my master's throat."

Larkin placed his finger on the point of the blade and forced it down. "There is no need. Your master is already dead."

"Dead?"

"As good as. Things are about to change here. You will be the ruler of this town. You will rule over the Romans and the Celts alike."

"Why would you help me?"

"Because I feel for those who are treated as inferiors. I am on the side of the underdog. You and I are brothers, united against tyranny."

Candle lowered his knife and held out his blood-stained hand. "We are brothers."

Larkin took his hand. "Now, I need your help. How can I get close to Commander Clodius Albinus?"

"Boethius will take you."

"Why would he?"

"You are a novelty. He will want to show you off."

"Will the commander grant him an audience?"

"Yes. My master has been helping the commander compose letters to persuade the emperor to name the town after him."

"Why should the commander want a town named after him?"

"The same reason that my master writes."

Larkin grinned. "These Romans want to defeat death but if

you do my bidding, I will help you claim victory over life."

The following day, as Candle had predicted, Boethius took Larkin to Albinus' villa. Candle walked behind, carrying the wrapped egg, as instructed by both his masters.

"How will I recognize this commander?" asked Larkin as they waited in a large, empty room.

"He will be the last to set foot inside. Before he enters, the room must be filled with people," replied Boethius. "Or, more like adorers to adore him,' he added wryly. "His advisors, cousins and aunts, some ambitious military men and other fawning sycophants. I notice he even has a dwarf these days. Watch now, here they come."

Just as Boethius had said, the room filled with people talking amongst themselves, moving into position like actors in a play. Clodius Albinus was the last to enter. He wore an ostentatious wreath on his head and held a bowl in one hand and a spoon in the other. He dipped the spoon in and tasted the contents of the bowl.

"Why, Mills, it's ice cold," he said.

"Yes, commander," replied a child-sized man. "Freezing is part of the process."

"That's the dwarf," Boethius whispered in Larkin's ear. "It seems he has made the commander a new dessert."

"And you say it is made from cow's milk?" said Albinus.

"Amongst other ingredients," said Mills.

"I like it. Make more."

The dwarf bowed. "I am pleased it meets with your satisfaction."

Larkin understood why the commander needed such an audience. Albinus was an unimaginably dull-looking man with a forgettable face and a regrettable squint. He looked at Larkin but addressed Boethius. "New find, Boethius?"

"I am a soothsayer," said Larkin.

"Of course you are," said Albinus, doubtfully. "Don't tell me, the marks on your temple are the fingerprints where the gods touched you."

"I cannot deny it," said Larkin, rubbing the bumps on his head.

"I presume you have a trick with which to impress us, Soothsayer?"

"A trick, no." Larkin leaned forward and spoke very quietly and quickly in Albinus' ear. "I have an offer. Employ me as an advisor and I will give you that which you most desire."

The commander's guards were quick to pull Larkin away and, for a moment, the entire room fell into tense silence until Albinus laughed. He shooed his guards away and placed an arm over Larkin's shoulder. Understanding that his part was now played, Boethius left with the rest of the room and returned home, with Candle and the egg.

3.

Albinus gave Larkin lodgings, enabling him to observe the day-to-day workings of a Roman commander. A steady stream of messengers from Rome arrived with orders and demands from the emperor. Albinus sent back these messengers with his replies, praising the emperor's wisdom and thanking him for his vigilance but, as far as Larkin could tell, not one of his brother's orders was acted upon.

A number of these messages concerned the name of the town. Albinus frequently made the case for naming it after

97

himself while his brother, just as frequently, refused to give permission and suggested naming it after himself.

"Where is my new advisor?" shouted Albinus.

"How may I assist, my commander?" asked Larkin.

"You promised me all that I desire."

"Yes, my commander. What would you have me do?"

"I want this stronghold named after me, and I can do nothing without my brother's permission."

"Why?" demanded Larkin. "He is not here."

Albinus looked at the dwarf. "Mills, here, advises me to be patient."

Mills bowed. "Good things come to those who wait and, after all, patience is a virtue, commander."

"Patience is a tool used by dictators to oppress their subjects," scoffed Larkin. "Why wait? You are Commander Clodius Albinus."

Albinus plucked a grape from a servant's tray. It looked distinctly old and wrinkled but he ate it none the less. "I like your directness, Larkin. Mills, leave us."

"As you desire."

Mills glanced at Larkin, then left. Once he was gone, Albinus linked arms with his new advisor. "If you really are what you say, then fulfill your promise to me."

"If the naming of the town is the most important thing to you then I will make it so, but surely this is not the limit of your ambition," said Larkin.

Albinus looked around the room. "Everybody out. I will speak to my soothsayer in private."

Once the room was cleared he turned to Larkin and said, "I wish to be emperor but my six brothers stand in my way – each as corrupt, wicked and weak as the next."

"Allow me." Larkin placed his fingertips on Albinus' forehead. The commander was presented with a vision in which he was stood on the great steps of the Roman Senate. He looked down and saw that he was dressed in the emperor's clothes. The crowd was chanting, "Hail Emperor Albinus! Hail Emperor Albinus!"

Larkin removed his hand and the vision vanished.

"You ... you ... you do have a gift," he said.

"That was the future, but you must do as I say to make it so."

"What must I do?"

"First you must send three of your strongest soldiers to Boethius' house and remove the large oval object that rests on a plinth in his dining room."

"How will they explain their actions to Boethius?"

"There will be no need. His slave, Candle works for me now. He will let them in. Once they have removed the egg, Boethius will cease to be a concern."

"It is a crime to steal from another Roman," said Albinus.

"It is not theft. The egg belongs to me."

"What if Boethius does not see it like that?"

"As I have said, he will give you no trouble once the egg is removed. But, a word of caution: tell your men they should not touch the egg directly if they value their lives."

"How will this help me become emperor?"

"The egg is everything. Control the egg and you control all life ... and all death."

4.

Clodius Albinus sat in the council chamber with Larkin the soothsayer and Mills the dwarf. "Dead?" said Albinus.

99

"Dead," replied Mills.

"Did they say the cause?" Albinus glanced guiltily at Larkin.

"The surgeon said Boethius had been dead for several days. Possibly an entire week," said Mills.

"But that is not possible. He was in this very room but a few days ago," replied Albinus.

"Intriguing, isn't it?" Mills was also looking at Larkin.

"Did he make any guess as to the cause of death?" asked Larkin.

"The only thing about which the surgeon was positive was that Boethius stopped breathing. Beyond that, he was unclear."

"Then there was no brutality?" said Albinus. "No injury or assault? After all, he did make a number of powerful enemies by doubting the existence of our gods."

"That's another interesting thing," said Mills. "According to that which he wrote before he died, he appeared to have found God."

"Which god?" asked Albinus.

"To use his words, the one true God," said Mills.

"Boethius, the great atheist, found religion?" Albinus laughed.

"Rather too late for that," said Larkin with a wry smile.

"It is never too late to repent one's sins and to beg for forgiveness. Redemption is always available to those who seek it." Mills spoke directly to Larkin.

Larkin turned to face the dwarf with renewed interest. "It is you."

Mills nodded.

"Interesting that you should choose this diminutive form." Larkin patted him on the head.

"Do not confuse size with strength."

"What are you two talking about?" asked Albinus.

"Silence, mortal." Larkin waved his hand, sending the commander into a trance. He turned back to Mills. "So this is how it begins. You are here to stop me."

"I did warn you I would follow you here," said the dwarf. "You want to force these simplistic life forms to bow down before you. I am here to show them another way."

"Force is the only thing these humans understand. These Romans have used their superior strength to force the inhabitants of this land to their knees. I will be the champion of the oppressed people."

"You are the champion of darkness. I will offer them light."

"Light, dark . . . Good, bad . . . Right, wrong. It's always extremes with you, isn't it?" said Larkin. He tapped Albinus' forehead, awakening him once more.

"Larkin, Mills," said Albinus. "What is going on? Do you two know each other?"

"We do, and your dwarf is a traitor," said Larkin. "He has confessed to me that he seeks to manipulate you so that he may rule over you."

Albinus looked at Mills. "Is this true?"

"You must decide who to believe," said Mills.

"Indeed you must," said Larkin. "But if you are to achieve greatness you must first put this poisonous dwarf to death."

"Will you not defend yourself, dwarf?" asked Albinus.

"I will not," said Mills. "I must trust your judgment."

"Very well," said Albinus. "Since you are accused and will not deny the accusations, I find you guilty. Larkin, send for my executioner."

"May I suggest crucifixion?" said Larkin. "A slower, more torturous death for such a traitor."

"Then so be it," said Albinus.

Mills held his palms up and made no protest as he was led away.

"Now, my commander," said Larkin, "you must take refuge in Boethius' house. Word has not yet got to Rome of his death. Assume his identity until all this is over and you will avoid the flurry of daggers that will come following your brothers' deaths. I have spoken with his slave. He will keep up the pretence and take care of you."

"My brothers are dead?"

"Not yet but soon. It is the only way to secure your ascension to the role of emperor."

"Then so be it," said Albinus. "I will become Boethius until your work is done. I am putting my fate in your hands, Larkin."

"It is not misplaced, I promise you. The time of Emperor Albinus is almost upon us."

5·

Once Albinus had moved into Boethius's house, Larkin had the egg transported to Rome. He spread word that Commander Clodius Albinus had sent the emperor a gift. He let it be known that this was a weapon that would bring death to all who stood in its way. The emperor was intrigued, but since Larkin had it taken to the senate, he was unable to keep his curious brothers away. All six brothers gathered to gaze upon the egg. All six touched it and experienced the revelations and knowledge it contained.

They retired to dine and discuss what they had learned but, while they were eating, Larkin snuck in and removed the egg from the building. As with Boethius, the brothers had died the moment they touched the alien object, but only when it was removed did their condition become evident. Discovering all six brothers dead, the senate guards accused the cooks and put them to death. A subsequent enquiry found the guards guilty and ordered their executions. Whoever had been directly responsible for the murders, it was assumed that the whole thing had been planned by Clodius Albinus. He was summoned to Rome to answer for his crimes.

It had been many years since Albinus had set foot in Rome so few recognized the man who came forward and threw himself onto the ground before the senate to plead his innocence. It is recorded that his plea lasted forty hours and forty minutes, during which time, many who heard it wept. By the end, every senator was convinced of two things: Clodius Albinus was innocent of the murder of his brothers, and he was the next rightful Emperor of Rome.

Those who had known him before his exile said that he had changed greatly. He was humbler, wiser, slightly taller, and had acquired two small protrusions at his temples. He was cunning and clever and so charismatic that his more eccentric orders were easily forgiven. When another exiled Roman, Boethius the scholar, was killed by his British slave, no one asked why the emperor pardoned the slave without enquiry or investigation. No one challenged his decisions to make Candle supreme governor of his native town then name the town *Larkin Mills*, after a soothsayer and dwarf so instrumental in the emperor's success.

The Dodgem Runners

1.

According to an old Roman law, Larkin Mills park
did not fall under the council's jurisdiction, making
it an ideal place for the steam fair to set up every summer.
The Fair Commandant was keen to avoid the health and safety lot because, although it was billed as the world's only full
steam-powered fun fair, in truth, it ran on the much cheaper
energy source of electric eels. The huge eel tank was kept out
of sight to maintain the illusion and to avoid any unwanted
attention from animal rights campaigners.

I became the eel keeper aged thirteen, when my father got
caught in a roll of barbed wire and ended up in the tank. I tried
not to think about how my usually safety-conscious father had
made such a silly mistake. Whether or not his death was an
accident was irrelevant since the whole thing had to be covered

up, as usual. The Fair Commandant told me that if the authorities found out, they would face crippling fines and I would be sent to the Institute for Parentally Impoverished but Talented Youngsters, which was a fancy name for the orphanage.

As eel keeper, it was my job to root through the local rubbish tips in search of electrical items to lob into the tank. These scavenging trips took me through the town so sometimes I ran errands for the other fair workers on my way. I had just picked up a set of curling tongs from the tip and a fresh batch of valve oil for Duncan, the nurse, when I spotted Mr. Morricone's Ice Cream Parlor. I had some money left over so I went in and ordered a Coconut Confession.

"You're from the fair," said Mr. Morricone.

Seeing my panicked expression he smiled and added, "Don't worry. You're most welcome in my shop. Although you will find my product quite different to those stingy scoops of flavored frost in stale cones you offer in the fair." He handed me the pot of ice cream. I took the small plastic spoon and tasted a mouthful. He was right. It was like eating a fluffy cloud. It might sound stupid but it tasted like hope itself.

"No matter what the Fair Commandant tells you, you are always welcome here," said Mr. Morricone.

I thanked him and stepped out of the ice cream parlor. A shaft of sunlight bounced off the office block opposite and illuminated me. I closed my eyes to enjoy its warmth but the moment was shattered when a hand landed on my shoulder. A policeman pulled the set of curling tongs from my bag and demanded "Where d'you nick this from then?"

The Fair Commandant had told us we should always run from the law, whether or not we had done something wrong, and so I wriggled free and legged it.

When I got back to the eel room I saw that the voltage was a little low in the tank so I chucked in the tongs and an old FM radio to ramp it up. I never did understand why electrical items had such an cffcct on the eels but a couple of medium-sized kitchen appliances could usually stimulate a day's worth of electricity. Every couple of months I had to empty the tank, clean the electrodes and patch up the thick wires that carried the electricity but, most of the time, I had very little to do so I would go and watch the dodgems.

The Dodgem Runners were the coolest of all the workers in the fair. It was down to them to keep the cars moving at all times. They had to leap onto the backs of moving cars, perform quick fixes and ensure that the connecting wire was touching the electrified top. Sometimes they had to reach over and grab the steering wheels to sort out a pile up created by an inexperienced driver. I loved watching them hop from car to car, as nimble as acrobats and as graceful as dancers. The beautiful display was made all the more exotic by the danger of their existence. With deadly electrical surges daily occurrences, electrocutions were common. Injury and incapacitation were all part of the job.

Every day, the Dodgem Runners stared danger in the face without flinching. The longest serving runner was Tony Fig, who had perfected the art of looking bored while performing an extraordinary triple jump followed by a twisting somersault just to fix a loose screw on the back of a connector.

Sprint was a tall ginger boy with a rat face and a high-pitched laugh. Gibbens had dark skin, bright eyes and always wore loose-fitting Hawaiian shirts open down to his naval. Monkey was the first ever girl runner. She had joined the fair a few years back as a moving target on the rifle range but had become a Dodgem Runner after beating Sprint's younger brother, Jackson, in the previous year's trials. They all worked for Old Mabel who rarely stepped out of the small cabin from which she kept watch and gave orders through the buzzing announcement system.

"CrAckle-BuzzzZZ . . . Drive in a clockwise direction . . . Keep your feet off the track . . . Stay inside the cars. HisssssSSS."

The paying punters assumed the speaker was making her words garbled and incomprehensible. Had Old Mabel ever stepped out of the cabin and addressed them directly, they would have learned that this was not the case. My dad told me once that when she was young she had fallen into the eel tank. Apparently the Fair Commandant himself fished her out but, since then, her hair stuck out in all directions, her eyes glowed bright blue and she spoke with that strange, distorted voice.

2.

It was my dream to join the Dodgem Runners but positions only became available when one of the four runners dropped out. I had been too young the last time, when a runner got caught in the middle of a head-on collision, but I wouldn't have beaten Monkey, anyway. She was amazing. There was no maximum age for a Dodgem Runner but, at nineteen, Tony Fig was the oldest a runner had ever got. The lucky ones walked away with only scars to remind them of the days on the dodgems. The unlucky ones didn't walk away at all. They were carried off.

The Fair Commandant didn't mind accidents, so long as there were no witnesses. He hated having to pay to have memories wiped clean, but *Complete Removals* vans were a common enough sight around the fair. I was throwing a blender into the eel tank when Jimmy from the Duck Shoot stall stepped into the eel room. "Gibbens has got a head cold," he said.

"Serious like?" I said.

"Just a sniffle."

I dropped the rest of the ball bearings in at once, sending sparks flying from the water in the electrified tank, then ran to the hospital tent.

A *head cold* in Fair speak meant an accident. A *sniffle* meant it was serious. A *paper cut* meant there had been a decapitation at the coconut shy. An *ingrowing toenail* meant an impaling at the House of Fun.

The hospital tent was situated behind the Ghost Train so that the screams of agony sounded like part of the ride. Gibbens was screaming as I entered. The bandage around his head was stained red. Duncan held him down while he writhed and swore.

"Morning, Ross," said Duncan causally. "Chuck us a syringe, would you? There's a pile on the table behind me."

"What happened?" I asked.

"Head injury," he said. "He got caught between two cars along the eastern ridge."

I picked up one of the syringes filled with the deep purple liquid and carried it over.

"No," cried Gibbens, desperately struggling to get free. "No, please! Get off me."

"Don't be silly. This will help," said Duncan. "Ross, do us a favor and stick it in, would you?"

"No, not that," begged Gibbens.

"It will take away the pain," said Duncan.

"No, Ross. No," said Gibbens. "Please. No."

"He doesn't know what he's saying. Head colds are always like this. You'd better get on with it. We don't want the Fair Commandant hearing this racket."

"Please don't, Ross. Drop me at the hospital," pleaded Gibbens. "I won't let on I'm from the fair."

"You know how it is, Gibbens," said Duncan. "No records, no hospitals. It's the fair way. Come on, Ross, hand it over."

Duncan was right. It was the fair way. Gibbens would have done the same in my place. I handed Duncan the syringe. He jabbed the needle into his leg and pushed the plunger. The strength vanished from Gibbens' body in an instant.

"Thanks," said Duncan. "Spread the word that there will be a display tonight."

It was steam fair tradition that anyone who died on duty was cremated and had their ashes sent up as fireworks. It was the closest fair folk were allowed to a funeral.

3.

Once Gibbens' remains had twirled and whirled in fizzing displays of exploding light, watched by a crowd of onlookers providing respectful oohs and aahs, the Fair Commandant removed his hat and made a speech to mark his passing.

"We remember the day Master Gibbens came into this world." He pulled on his goatee beard thoughtfully. "His mother was forced to close the Whirling Dervish ride early to give birth. We didn't mind about the loss of revenue. We knew Gibbens would earn his keep in time. That time was shorter than many but longer than some, and it means that Old Mabel needs a replacement runner. Should you wish to take his place on the dodgems, Old Mabel asks that you step onto the track barefoot at midnight for the trials. But, let us add a word of caution: the life of a Dodgem Runner is not for everyone. Nor is the death, come to think of it." He chuckled. "Now, raise your glasses to the memory of Master Gibbens."

Once Gibbens' life had been toasted, Sprint placed an arm around his brother and said, "Jackson missed out last time but he'll be a Dodgem Runner by tomorrow."

"I'm ready," said Jackson.

Jackson spent the whole evening trying to intimidate any likely rivals, but obviously didn't consider me one because he looked surprised when, at the strike of midnight, I stepped out onto the dodgem track. We looked into each other's eyes. Jackson wore something between a sneer and smile. I tried not to show fear. A cold breeze blew through the fair and I felt my toes tingle.

"The job is mine, Eel Boy," said Jackson. "Everyone knows that. It's not too late to get off and wriggle back to the tank room where you belong."

"Don't call me that," I said.

"Eel Boy? That's your name, isn't it? Well, you don't worry me, Eel Boy."

"I seem to remember you weren't worried by Monkey," I said pointedly.

Jackson spat. "I wasn't ready. I am now. I've been training every day since then for this."

"Then isn't it lucky that Gibbons got that head cold," I said. "I don't suppose you had anything to do with that accident?"

"As I heard it, you were the one who handed the essence to Duncan," said Jackson.

I tried not to think about the look of helpless desperation on Gibbons' face as the poison entered his bloodstream.

"KhahHHhh ... Jackson Tooley, Ross Fairchild." Old Mabel's voice came over the crackling speaker. "Today we said goodbye to runner Gibbens, bringing our numbers down to three ... WoOORCH."

Tony, Sprint and Monkey took their places at the edge of the track. They were all dressed in black.

"HisZzZZz ... A team of four runners is required to keep the dodgems running," continued Old Mabel. "Every fault must be fixed. Keep the cars flowing. Keep the cars moving. Stay in the same direction. Movement is money ... FuhfuhffzzZZZzz."

Sprint, Monkey and Tony Fig each picked up a long black pole and hopped onto a static dodgem car.

"PopZiZiZzzzzZ ... A runner's life is not an easy option," warned Old Mabel. "You must conquer your fear and embrace the danger. This is your last chance to step off the track and back out ... KerSHIZZZzzZ."

Neither of us moved.

"GuuuUH ... So be it," said Mabel. "Tonight you will experience hardship, danger and excitement. You will get bumps, bruises, scratches and cuts. By the end, one of you will be one of us. Now jump ... CrAckLE."

The power came on. Distorted music blasted out of the speakers. I felt a light buzz in the soles of my feet and leapt up. I grabbed onto a moving car. The colored lights flashed and the live electrical current hissed and fizzed.

"FuZIZ ... The current is on maximum. That's ten eels of electricity flowing," said Mabel. "These cars are your only way of avoiding being burned to a crisp.... pOp."

I watched the three Dodgem Runners jumping from car to

car. Bricks had been gaffer-taped to the accelerators and ropes tied to hold the steering wheels in place.

"HiIssSs ... The first challenge will test your speed," said Mabel. "The rules are simple. Stay moving. Spend any longer than two seconds on one car and you are fair game ... FiZZle."

Tony swung his stick at my legs. I jumped up to avoid it and landed on a car whizzing past in the other direction.

"Ccccc ... Only one person to a car. Step onto your opponent's car and you will be disqualified," said Mabel. "If you both avoid disqualification by the end of the ride the winner will be the one with the fewest fouls incurred ... BooOsh!"

Another stick came out of nowhere. I jumped to a blue one but Jackson's car nudged it and I had to stretch my arm to grab the connector by my fingertips.

The music pulsed through my veins as I found my stride. It wasn't easy. I needed to keep an eye on the cars, the runners' poles and Jackson. I had to think three or four jumps ahead but also second-guess where Jackson was heading. With only two seconds per car it was an extremely narrow percentage of error.

"What's wrong, Ross? First time you've played this game?" yelled Jackson.

I felt a sharp pain on the back of my leg. I jumped but the force of the blow threw me off balance and my toe touched the track. Pain surged through me and a klaxon sounded.

"KhhhSwISHhh ... Ross incurs one foul ... FiZZLe," said Mabel.

"That's not fair," I protested. "I got hit but I wasn't on that car over two seconds."

"Runners don't play fair," said Sprint, close behind. It had been his pole. He was looking out for his brother.

My only hope now was to get Jackson disqualified. It wasn't going to be easy with his brother helping him, but I was going to have to stop playing to survive and start playing to win. I watched Jackson, trying to work out where he was heading. Red car, blue car, yellow car, green ... If I could jump faster than Jackson, then I could get to the green car first, meaning he would have nowhere to land.

I sped up, making big unpredictable jumps, keeping that green car in my sights. I couldn't tell whether Jackson had guessed my plan but he sped up too. Blue car to the yellow car ... The black-clad runners circled like crows. One more to go. I leapt but, once again, Sprint took a swing at me. The pole hit me square in the face and both Jackson and I landed on the green car. The final klaxon sounded and Old Mabel switched off the power.

Everything stopped.

"WeOorchHHH ... Runners, whose foot landed first? TshhHh," asked Old Mabel.

"I wasn't near enough to say for sure," said Tony, "but it looked to me like Jackson's foot came down first."

"I thought it was Ross," said Monkey quickly.

Jackson scowled at her.

"FuZZZ ... Then it looks like Sprint has the deciding vote... ChIZZZ," said Old Mabel.

"Jackson landed first," said Sprint without hesitation.

I didn't bother contesting the decision. There was no point.

"Jackson wins the first trial," said Mabel. "The next trial will take place on top of Bottle Moth Hill. Contestants, you have ten minutes to be there."

4.

Even though I put on my shoes and raced to Bottle Moth Hill as quickly as possible, the others all beat me there. They waited until I took my place next to Jackson, then Monkey stepped forward.

"Runners need quick hands," she said. "When the winner of tonight's trials is required to perform a repair job on a car tomorrow, you'll have to keep that car going while others are crashing into you from all directions. A Dodgem Runner needs to be quick enough to catch a flame." With one hand she took out a matchbox and match then flicked it so that it ignited and went out in a second.

With lightning reactions, Jackson snatched it out of the air. "If we have to repair cars then the test should be repairing cars," he said, revealing the blackened match in his palm.

"The second trial is always decided by the newest runner," said Tony.

Monkey lit another match and held its flame up to Jackson's face. "And that's me."

"Not for long," he replied, unflinchingly. "I was born for this."

"Being a Dodgem Runner is not a right." Tony blew out the match. "You will have to earn your place as one of us, Jackson."

"Or Ross will," said Monkey.

Sprint and Jackson laughed.

"We're wasting time," said Tony. "Let's get on."

"So what do we do?" I asked.

Sprint handed us a jam jar each.

"Bottle moths," said Monkey. "He who catches the most moths by the time the klaxon goes wins the trial."

"Easy," said Jackson, tucking the jar into his belt.

"When you hear the klaxon, you need to be back on the ground in less than a minute before a second klaxon goes off. If you're not, you'll be disqualified no matter how many you've caught."

I pushed the jar into my jeans pocket.

"Some say bottle moths can smell fear," said Monkey. "Let's see if this is true. Now, if you're ready, then get set, and go."

I have always been a good tree climber. It wasn't long before I was high up where the branches swayed in the breeze. Jackson was three trees to my left. Tony, Sprint and Monkey were climbing too. I wondered who was in charge of the klaxon. Had Old Mabel actually left her cabin? Once I drew level with the glowing blue insects, I stopped. I pulled the jar from my pocket and watched a moth a couple of inches from my head. I was trying to identify a pattern in its movements, but it was too erratic. I heard Jackson slam the lid down on his jar.

"Yes," he hissed.

I didn't turn. I knew he was probably just trying to goad me into making a mistake. I began to unscrew the lid on my jar but the moth flew higher so I slipped it back in my pocket. However, I must have put the lid on badly because it slipped from the jar and dropped to the ground.

"How many you got so far, Ross?" asked Jackson. "I'm about to get my second."

I felt sick to my stomach. Even if I went back down, there was no chance of finding the lid but, without it, how could I hold in the moths? I watched Jackson open his jar to catch his second, only for the first to fly out.

"Drat."

I wanted to feel pleased about Jackson's mistake but, with no lid, I had already lost.

Sprint appeared on a tree behind me and whispered, "Time to give up, eel boy. No lid. No hope."

Could Sprint have sabotaged me again? Had it been his hand that knocked the lid off as I tucked the jar into my pocket? Sprint wanted his brother on the team. He wanted me to give up. For a moment, I considered it.

Then I heard Monkey's voice whisper in my ear.

"Don't look for a pattern. They don't choose where they go."

I took a deep breath and shut out every sound except that of the fluttering moth wings. I allowed my eyes to lose focus so that the pattern of blue light became blurred. I remembered my father saying that bottle moths only live for a week. Was that why they moved so fast? Were they desperate to make the most of their short lives?

"They're like us," said Monkey.

"Yes."

I understood. The moths weren't making decisions. They were responding to their surroundings: the breeze, the sway of the leaves, Jackson and I trying to catch them. They were instinctive and reactive, just as Dodgem Runners had to be. Finally realizing what I needed to do, I moved my hands slowly. I raised the jar, then placed my hand over the top. When I looked inside, I had caught one.

I lifted the jar to inspect it. The captured moth flew up to my hand and I felt a twinge of pain.

"Ow." I snatched my hand away.

Sprint laughed. "No one ever told you, Ross? Bottle moths sting."

I slammed my hand back but it was too late. The jar was empty. Once again, I climbed as fast as I could until I drew level with the buzzing creatures.

I found a part where the trunk forked in two. I wedged myself securely to free up both hands. Once again, I moved my hands as slowly as I could manage. I closed my eyes, lifted the jar slowly, and lowered my other hand to cover the top. When I looked inside the jar, it was glowing brightly. I didn't know how many were there but my hand was in agony as the trapped bottle moths stung the fleshy barrier that stood between them and freedom.

The klaxon sounded. Jackson instantly started climbing down, but what could I do? Even if I could make it down using my elbows there was no way I would get to the ground before the second klaxon sounded. If I lost this trial, it was over. I looked down. The Dodgem Runners stared death in the face every day. This was my first time. The question was whether it would be my last.

I stepped off the branch.

An uninterrupted fall from that height would have killed me the moment I hit the ground but I picked a path dense with branches. As I fell I hit branch after branch. Each one hurt but also slowed me down enough that by the time I felt the impact of the ground on my knees, it didn't break my legs.

I dropped to the ground and felt its dampness seep through my trousers. Laughter rang in my ears. The second klaxon sounded. I slowly rose to my feet. My legs shook like jelly but my hands refused to release my prize.

Monkey took Jackson's jar first. She removed the lid and counted the bottle moths that flew out.

"One, two, three, four ... five," she said.

Jackson grinned.

Monkey looked at me, my hand still covering the top of the jar.

"Are you ready?" she asked.

I nodded, unsure whether I could speak.

"Lift your hand off," said Monkey.

I did as I was told and the moths flew out. My vision was still too blurred from the fall to count them but I heard Monkey's voice. "One, two, three, four, five, six, seven."

I felt dizzy.

"Ross wins," said Tony. "It's one all. Both of you, follow me for the final trial."

5.

Sprint did not look happy with his brother as they followed Tony out of the park but I couldn't hear their conversation because I was walking next to Monkey.

"You did well," she said. "This could still be yours."

"What's the last trial?" I asked.

"Tony hasn't told us," she replied. "But you can bet it will be dangerous. For my final trial, Jackson and I went head to head in a train-hopping competition. He's lucky to be alive."

"Why do they have to be so dangerous?"

"Because that's our life. Have you thought about why you want this?"

"It's all I've ever wanted," I said.

"Why? Because it looks cool? You think danger is cool? You think death is cool?"

I thought about my father's pained screams as he thrashed around in the eel tank. I remembered the dying light in Gibbens' eyes as the poison devoured him from the inside. "No, it's not about being cool," I said. "I want to join because the runners are a team. Whenever I watch you, you work together.

You trust each other. You rely on each other. I want to be a part of something like that."

Monkey draped an arm around my shoulder, her hand dangling near my cheek. "That's a good reason, Ross."

"What about you? Why did you join?" I asked.

She smiled. "Me? I just thought it looked cool."

It hurt when I laughed.

"Whatever it is, this last trial will be proper dangerous," she said.

"Dodgem Runners aren't supposed to feel fear," I replied.

"You say that like it's a good thing." Monkey pulled out the matchbox and handed it to me. I turned it over in my hands and read the back. It said, FIRE KILLS –KEEP AWAY FROM CHILDREN. "Fear is there to keep you safe," said Monkey.

"The Fair Commandant says nothing is really safe," I said.

Monkey took back her matchbox and withdrew her arm. "You grew up in the fair, didn't you, Ross?"

"Yes."

"I didn't. I had another life. I had a real name. I lived in Larkin Mills with my father."

"So why did you come here?"

"My house was destroyed in a fire. My father was inside."

"I'm sorry."

"Why? It wasn't *your* fault."

I didn't want to ask what she meant by that. Instead I said, "Why did you join the fair?"

"I joined because life in Larkin Mills is cruel and unjust but everyone pretends it isn't. In the fair, we don't pretend."

"Except to the customers," I said. "I don't think anyone has ever hooked a duck on the Hook-a-duck stall."

Monkey laughed. Tony stopped on the pedestrian bridge

that crossed the road, separating the park from the town. He jumped up onto the barrier and raised his hands. "The Larkin Mills ring road," he said. "The third most dangerous road in Europe, boasting a higher casualty rate than the bubonic plague and the only major road in Britain on which you have to drive on the right." Tony sprung up onto his toes, displaying no fear that he might fall. Below, the headlights whizzed past.

"So what's the challenge then?" asked Jackson. "Traffic dodging? Easy."

Tony ignored the interruption. "For the final challenge you'll need to be light on your feet and fast with your hands. By now, you're both tired, but Dodgem Runners can't afford to get tired. Old Mabel has us working ten-hour shifts and most accidents occur at the end of the day."

Jackson nudged me and whispered, "I ain't even tired."

I was shattered. My body felt like it would collapse in on itself any second. I was covered with scratches and bruises from the fall but the exhaustion and the pain were numbed by the adrenaline coursing through my body.

"For this challenge you'll need to conquer your fear," said Tony. "Take a look down. What do you see?"

We peered over the edge. "Traffic," said Jackson.

"Look more closely," said Tony.

"An open manhole," I said.

"Correct," said Tony. "It leads to the Larkin Mills sewers. You will each drop down past the traffic, through the manhole into the sewer. This far from the town center it is fast flowing and reasonably clean but it will get dirtier the further you go."

"So what? We have to swim through filth?" said Jackson.

"FZZZzzzz ... Not swim. Surf ... FfFfuh," said a distorted voice.

We turned around to find Old Mabel standing behind us, holding a surfboard under each arm. Her eyes glowed as brightly as a pair of trapped bottle moths.

"KKkchcch ... I expect these back in one piece ... THthTH," She handed us the surfboards.

"Larkin Mills sewers are tidal," said Tony. "You're racing to the aqueduct. Ross, you collected the most bottle moths so you get to go first. There are more twists and turns in the sewers than a tank of eels but if you take more rights than lefts then you should end up somewhere along the aqueduct. We'll meet you there. The first one to the end grate wins."

"It's not fair that he gets to go first," said Jackson. "I won the first trial."

"FZZzzH ... If you get through this one, you'll learn not to question orders ... ZzZZ," said Old Mabel.

"Good luck." Monkey winked at me.

"I'll be right behind you," said Jackson.

I climbed up onto the railing and looked down at the stream of headlights whizzing past. Was this really what I wanted? A life of fear? A life that could end at any point because of a silly mistake? I gripped the surfboard.

"Get a move on," said Sprint.

"Conquer your fear," said Tony.

I waited until a huge juggernaut rattled underneath, then dropped, aiming for the manhole. The fall was the single most intense experience of my life. The rush of the wind, the sound of the traffic, the approach of a headlight, then the darkness of the sewer and the splash of the icy cold water. I plunged down and came splashing back up. I scrabbled to get out of the water and onto the surfboard. Something solid brushed against my hand. I tried not to think about what it could be.

For a moment, I lay on the surfboard, wondering what happened next, then I heard the rush of water. A wave was coming. I jumped onto my feet as it hit and tried desperately to keep my balance. The suddenness of the movement took me by surprise but I managed to stay upright. The only light came from the streetlamps through gaps in the manholes above. I stretched my arms out wide and felt the rough edges of the tunnel walls. This made my fingertips sore but it meant I could control which way I went and stay to the right. I could hear Jackson howling with excitement but the sound stopped when the wave passed and the water calmed.

"Ross?" Jackson's voice echoed down the tunnel. "Ross. Something's down here."

"Very funny," I replied.

"I'm serious." Jackson sounded different. Scared.

I saw something move under the water.

"Ross?" shouted Jackson. "What is it? What's down here?"

I had heard the rumors about what lurked in Larkin Mills sewers but had assumed they were just that. I watched the dark shape break the surface. When I saw the fin I understood it was true.

"Sewer sharks," I said, too quietly for Jackson to hear over the sound of another approaching wave. I jumped up onto my feet, as desperate to escape the shark as to catch the wave. It was no longer about winning the trial. It was about getting out with our lives. The surfboard rocked violently as the rush of water propelled me forward. The further I got into the heart of the sewer, the smellier it grew. The horrific stench hit me as the wave died away and I dropped down into the water. It was impossible to stay standing on the board when it was calm. The putrid water stung the cuts, scratches and scrapes I had got up on Bottle Moth Hill. If I was bleeding, it would attract the attention of the sharks. I tried to keep my limbs out of the water but couldn't keep the surfboard still. I could see a large shark-shaped shadow under the water, swimming towards me. All I could do was watch as a huge head reared up. Rows of razor-sharp teeth caught the light and I realized that fear was no longer of any use. I was beyond fear. In that moment, I understood that death wasn't a choice. Everything else in life was, but death was inevitable. It was just a matter of timing. I closed my eyes and waited.

The next thing I heard was the sound of a shark being punched on the nose. I opened my eyes and saw Jackson floating next to me. "I saw it in a thing on television once," he said. "You're supposed to punch them on the nose. Or was that bears?"

"Don't say there are bears down here too," I said.

He smiled. "I mean, why are there sharks in the sewers?"

"I think it was something to do with a military experiment gone wrong. Or something to do with the council. I can't remember which."

"This town is insane."

We looked at each other and laughed so hard I thought my sides would split. The uncontrollable hysteria that gripped us felt good and I mourned its passing when the laughter died away.

"Thanks for saving me," I said.

"Well, I might want to beat you but I don't want to see you eaten by a shark in a sewer," said Jackson.

Before I could respond, a colossal wave hit. It was the biggest yet and I was dragged away from Jackson. For a moment, I lost my grip on the surfboard but I got hold of it again and managed to clamber on as the wave transported me down the network of gloomy tunnels. The concentration demanded to stay upright removed all thoughts of the sharks. I understood why Dodgem Runners performed such insane stunts. The focus required to perform death-defying acts blocked out everything else. They were so immersed in their survival that they could forget all of the pain of life.

When the wave died away, I wiped my eyes and saw that I was in a wider tunnel with a grate at one end. On the other side of the grate was the night sky. It was the aqueduct. The end was in sight. I paddled fast.

"Hello, Eel Boy." Sprint stood at the side of the tunnel on a narrow path.

"Leave me alone," I said. "Jackson's probably out already, anyway."

"No, he's not." Sprint held a bucket in one hand and a large pair of plastic tongs in the other. "Jackson took a wrong turn. He's at least five minutes behind you. If you get to that grate you've won. I can't have that. I've been training up my brother since he was crawling around in nappies," said Sprint. "Go back to throwing toasters in a tank, Eel Boy."

"The trials are designed to find the best person for the job," I replied.

"And so they will." Sprint reached into the bucket with the tongs and pulled out a wriggling electric eel, fizzing and sending off sparks. It was my biggest female. "How does it work then, Eel Boy? What happens if I drop this fella in with you?"

"It will create a localized current and I'll fry," I said.

"And Jackson will win?" said Sprint.

"And Jackson will win," I admitted.

"So?" said Sprint. "Aren't you going to beg me not to drop it?

Aren't you going to tell me you'll let him win if I don't? Aren't you going to plead for your life?"

"No," I said. "If you're going to drop it, then go ahead. I'm not scared any more."

The light of the moon vanished as Tony appeared at the grate at the end of the tunnel. "Well, Ross Fairchild. It looks like we have our new runner," he said.

"Well done, Ross," said Monkey, joining Tony on the other side of the grate.

"No," said Sprint. "He hasn't won yet."

"Put the eel down," said Tony.

"You're not the boss," said Sprint.

"Ross, get out of the water," said Monkey.

I swam with all my might and grabbed the side but Sprint was already releasing the eel. That would have been how I died, had one of the larger sharks not spotted the tantalizing bait being dangled. The shark shot out of the water, eager to feast on the eel. It bit into the eel, and took with it Sprint's arm. I hoisted myself out of the sewer as the shark crashed down into the water, followed by Sprint, who screamed as he fell into the electrified blood bath of filth.

I couldn't bear to look but Monkey and Tony watched with interest as Sprint was torn apart, cooked and drowned in the most horrific death imaginable. I was unsure how long it was before Jackson appeared.

"What's happened?" he asked.

"Congratulations," said Tony. "To both of you."

"Both of us?" said Jackson. "But who won?"

"It turns out there were two positions to fill," said Monkey.

"What? Where's my brother? Where's Sprint?" asked Jackson.

No one answered but Ross heard Old Mabel's voice say. "KhhCH ... Looks like there will be fireworks again tomorrow night, my runners ... WwWhhHHrrWWW."

The klaxon sounded twice, signifying the end of the trials and the appointment of two new runners.

I tried to process all I had witnessed. I had seen the look in Monkey's eyes as she watched Sprint die. It wasn't that the Dodgem Runners were unafraid of death. They were obsessed with it.

The Girl Who Noticed Things

1.

REGGIE SANDALS was a girl who noticed things. She didn't know if she noticed more things than other people because she wasn't inside other people's heads and she had never been good at guessing what other people were thinking. Maybe everyone noticed as much as she did. If they did, she wondered if their heads got all clogged up with it too. The thoughts in Reggie's head got so jumbled and confused that she took to writing them down on scraps of paper instead.

The spider's web on the shed is made from 324 strands. Dad's bellybutton fluff is always red. Mum's is always blue. I do not have belly button fluff.
The man on the radio said the word 'fantastic' seven times while I ate breakfast this morning.

Reggie found that writing things down helped, but soon learned not to leave the notes around the house. She noticed that sometimes her observations made her parents angry or sad, or both angry and sad.

Dad arrived home at 1.24 a.m. last night.
Mum cried for 3 minutes and 12 seconds at breakfast.
Sometimes milk lasts longer than its best before date.

She didn't know why her dad tore up this note and shouted at her but to avoid it happening again Reggie found an empty exercise book. She called the book *MY BOOK OF NOTICED THINGS*. Under this she wrote the words *STRICTLY CONFIDENTAIL*. She wrote the letters out carefully in stencils before noticing the spelling mistake.

The word confidential contains 12 letters, 5 of which are
vowels.
The spider's web on the shed has caught one fly so far.
Mum and Dad shouted at each other for 2 hours and 14
minutes tonight.
Mum cried in her room tonight. (I don't know for how
long as the door was locked and she is very good
at crying quietly.)
Today someone took away the SOLD sign from the
house across the road.

The house across the road had been for sale for as long as Reggie could remember. Its doors and windows were boarded up. Her dad told her it had stayed empty so long because there had been a fire there once and it was a big project to make it habitable again. She was excited by the prospect of new neighbors to watch because she had noticed most of the things to notice about most of the people in her street. Reggie spent a lot of time staring out of her bedroom window. It helped distract her from all the shouting and crying downstairs. She had a television in her room, which she turned on to block out the sound and to pretend to watch if one of them came into the room unannounced. Apparently, staring out of the window was *not normal*, while staring at a television was. Reggie had noticed that adults got upset when children did things that were considered *not normal*, but since no one had thought to write a book of what did and didn't fit into this category, Reggie found it very hard to understand which was which. Sometimes she added *normal/not normal* comments to the things she had noticed.

> *The postman comes to our house between 11.00 and 11.14 every morning. Normal.*
> *Next door's cat always walks on our wall but never enters our garden. Normal.*
> *When Dad arrives home he sits in the car for between 30 seconds to 2 minutes before getting out. Sometimes he is on the phone. Sometimes he is not. Not normal.*

It was while looking out of the window that Reggie noticed the blue van stop outside the house across the road. A man wearing a red woollen hat stepped out. He looked up at the house, then took a ladder from the back of the van. He placed the ladder against the side of the house, checked it was steady, then climbed up onto the roof. He took his time and climbed all the way to the top of the roof, then dropped down inside the chimney.

Reggie decided that this was probably a *not normal* way to enter a house. Her bedroom door opened. With the hall light on, her mother stood silhouetted in the doorway. When she stepped inside, Reggie could make out her blotchy red eyes. She smiled unconvincingly and said, "You should turn off the TV now. It's late."

Reggie did as she was told. "A man just entered the house across the road through the chimney," she said.

"I hope he didn't double-park his reindeer."

"He didn't have reindeer. He arrived in that van."

Her mother sighed. "You need to understand that no matter what happens, your father and I love you very, very much."

"You don't need to say very twice," said Reggie. "It's tautological."

Her mother ruffled her hair. "Clever girl."

"What if it's a burglar? I mean, the man with the ladder."

"Reggie, darling," said her mother. "The house across the road has been empty for years. What would they steal?"

Reggie had noticed that adults often asked questions that didn't require answers. They were called rhetorical questions and they were sometimes hard to identify. She suspected her mother's question was intended to be rhetorical, but Reggie still thought it deserved to be answered.

The man spent 46 minutes in the house before leaving the way he came. Not normal.
He put the ladder down, but left it by the house, then got back in the van and drove away. Not normal.
My mother is not interested in this man. Not normal.

The next time the man came to the house he was driving a much larger vehicle with an extendable arm on the back. Reggie had heard these vehicles described as cherry pickers, although, watching this one, it occurred to her that it was a very large piece of equipment to use to pick something as small as a cherry. She watched the man get into the back and struggle with the controls to raise himself up to the roof. Once he was level with the chimney, he began lowering crates inside. Reggie noticed one of her neighbors walking his dog. He paused to look at the truck but didn't notice the activity around the chimney.

2.

The man in the van returned the following morning and Reggie resolved to ask him what he was doing and whether entering a house through the chimney was *normal* or *not normal*. Maybe it was one of those things that adults did which only seemed strange to children, like watching the news, eating olives or staring into estate agent's windows.

The man was checking the ladder's stability when she coughed, and said, "Excuse me."

He turned to look at her. He had small, dark eyes. "Yes?" he said.

"I've noticed that most other people use the front doors to enter their houses, except for Mr. Hashmi at number twelve, who uses the one round the back."

The man looked confused. "I've observed that too. Not about Mr. Hashmi, I mean, but that most people use their doors."

"So why do you use the chimney?"

"This is no ordinary house," he said.

"Do you mean because it's boarded up?" asked Reggie.

"Yes and no. I'm Professor Priestly. Would you like to see inside?"

"I think so," she replied.

"Are you afraid of heights?"

"Only two."

"I'm sorry?"

Reggie never intentionally confused people but Professor Priestly was by no means the first person to look at her the way he did.

"So far I've been afraid of two heights. One was the Eiffel Tower in Paris. The other was a tree in Wales that didn't have a name. I can't say if I will be afraid on top of your house until I'm there."

"You're an interesting girl. What is your name?"

"Reggie Sandals, though most people call me Reggie. No one calls me Regina, which is the name on my birth certificate. I think I'd like to find out if I am scared by going up the ladder."

The man pulled out a piece of paper from the front seat of the van. "Would you mind signing this?" he asked.

He handed her the form and a ballpoint. Reggie read it before filling in the blanks.

I [INSERT NAME HERE] accept full responsibility for my actions and accept that the Larkin Mills Department of Planning is not in any way culpable for anything that should happen to me while on the property named above. This includes injury, accident, loss of limb, lack of perspective, ingrowing toenails, bunions or death.

Reggie signed underneath and handed it back to Professor Priestly.

"The Department of Planning," she said. "What are you planning for?"

"Eventualities."

"So you work for the council?"

"Yes, they pay for all this. I'm a marine biologist," he said.

"Is that fish?" she said.

"Yes, fish," he replied.

Reggie followed him up the ladder to the roof where she discovered she was a little scared of this height. She clambered up the roof tiles to the chimney and looked down.

"There's a ladder on the inside," said Professor Priestly.

She climbed down into the darkness. Professor Priestly followed her inside. He pulled a cord and a light came on. The attic was packed with barrels, wetsuits and diving equipment. Professor Priestly opened a wooden trapdoor in the floor and revealed something which, at first, looked like a mirror. He touched its surface, creating ripples.

"The house is full of water," said Reggie.

He nodded. "Now you see why one must enter this house through the roof."

"How did you fill a house with water?"

"It's not so difficult. We had the place made watertight, then turned the taps on. There is a flushing mechanism in the cellar that sends the dirty water down the sewer and replaces it with clean water from the reservoir.

"Why did you fill a house with water?"

"So I can study my subjects in a controlled environment. And what could be more controlled than a semi-detached house in a suburban street?"

"What are your subjects?" Reggie dipped her hand in the water.

"Sharks. Fascinating creatures," said Professor Priestly.

Reggie withdrew her hand quickly.

Professor Priestly prised open a barrel, releasing the potent smell of fish. He carefully tipped the barrel so that the top layer of fish slid out and into water. The water rippled, splashed over the side, then discolored. The tip of a tail appeared, then vanished.

"Are they dangerous?" asked Reggie.

"Potentially." Professor Priestly picked up a wetsuit from a rack. Reggie noticed the letters *LMDP* on the front.

"Are you going in?" said Reggie.

"I'm training them. I can hardly do that from up here."

"I've heard of people training dolphins but never sharks."

"Dolphins are fine for tricks but, as hunters, sharks have no rivals. Now, excuse me." Professor Priestly stepped behind a screen to change into the wetsuit.

"Aren't you worried?" asked Reggie.

"Not in the slightest," he replied. "These sharks think of me as their family and a shark will not harm its family."

"How many are down there?"

"Five at the moment, but it's the mating season soon so there'll be more on the way. Now, I'm sorry but I must get to work. You're welcome to stay or go as you please."

Professor Priestly took a step and dropped down into the water. Alone in the attic, Reggie made a mental note of the things she noticed about the room.

There is a rack of identical black wetsuits with the initials LMPD on the front.

The oxygen tanks are green and have LARKIN MILLS COUNCIL USE ONLY printed on the side.
There are several sizes of wetsuit including one that would fit me.
When you shine a torch into the water you can see the wallpaper in the room below. It has pictures of old competitive basket weaving players printed on it.

When Professor Priestly climbed out of the water he pulled off his mask and said, "Yes, I thought you would still be here."

"Why does the council pay you to keep sharks in a house?"

"It's a council house so it didn't cost them anything. Also, we felt an aquarium would attract too much attention."

"What are they doing down there?'

"At the moment they're all in the kitchen because Mrs. Harte next door is cooking dinner."

"Do you mean that the sharks can smell the food?"

"Unlikely, but it's not just blood sharks can smell. Did you know that sharks can detect electricity? It's a hunting skill because their prey give off electrical currents. The sharks are in the kitchen because of Mrs. Harte's blender."

"What if they got through the wall?"

"Reinforced glass, extra thick walls. Not a chance."

"Do the neighbors know they have sharks living next door?"

Professor Priestly towelled his hair dry. "No. I'm not sure they would appreciate a family of sharks next door. Not in my street, they would say. Not in this kind of place. This is a neighborhood for nice people, not blood-thirsty sea creatures. That sort of thing. Here in suburbia, people can be extremely narrow-minded."

"So why are you telling me?" asked Reggie.

"Because you showed an interest," said Professor Priestly simply. "It's the first requirement of a scientist. It's what most people lack."

"I notice things," said Reggie.

"That's good but it's not enough. A true scientist does more than notice. You need to come up with theories about the things you notice, then put those theories to the test. A scientist must infer from his or her observations. You must learn to draw conclusions."

3.

Reggie had been visiting the shark house for two weeks when she arrived home to find her father staring at a television show in which two members of the public had to bake cupcakes in a room slowly being filled with toxic gas.

"Reggie," he said, apparently unable to look away from the screen. "Where have you been?"

From the armchair where he was sat, it would have only have taken a turn of the head to see her climbing down from the chimney of the house across the road.

"I've been in a house full of sharks."

"Haven't you got homework or something?" said her father.

Reggie didn't point out that she didn't have any homework because it was the holidays. Since her parents had started arguing so much, they had noticed less and less about anything other than themselves. She went upstairs to her room and wrote down all the things she had noticed and learned that day.

Sharks can smell blood from a quarter of a mile away. Some sharks are sociable and have communities. Professor Priestly prefers the company of sharks to most humans because, he says, it's easier to understand what sharks want.

She enjoyed her time in the attic but she knew that the real interest was down in the house. The next day, she said what was on her mind.

"I want to go with you. I'd like to go down into the house."

Professor Priestly considered this. "I'd have to take a harpoon, just in case."

"You mean, you'll let me?" said Reggie excitedly.

"You'll need a wetsuit."

"You have one that will fit me. Will it be dangerous?"

"Very little worth doing is totally devoid of danger. You'd better bring a torch too. It's dark down there."

"I'm not worried about that."

Even a dark house filled with water and sharks was preferable to her home. On the rare occasions her parents were in the same room they communicated entirely through her.

"Reggie, please ask your mother what she did with the remote control."

"Reggie, please tell your father that he had it last."

"Reggie, please inform your mother that she is wrong about that."

After a lesson about how to use the breathing equipment, Reggie dropped down into the water. Professor Priestly had explained that the sharks only came upstairs at feeding times, which gave her time to get used to the water before she met one. She swam down into the room. Much of the wallpaper was singed and blackened and had peeled off the walls. It moved like seaweed as she waved her hand over it. In the torchlight, Reggie could make out lines on the wall where a parent had marked the height of a child. Floating up by a lampshade made from a wheel hub were two stuffed squirrels in ballet positions. Professor Priestly caught her attention and pointed down. Reggie nodded.

She followed him through the doorway into the landing where there were more peculiar items. She spotted a motorcycle engine and a Russian space suit as Professor Priestly led her down the staircase into the hallway. The house was identical to her own in layout. She caught sight of her first shark by the hat-stand at the bottom of the stairs. It swam straight towards her, only just avoiding a collision. Reggie had to remind herself to keep breathing as the huge fish brushed past her ear. She followed Professor Priestly into the living room where two more sharks were circling a chandelier. At first, she was alarmed by their dead eyes but, the more time she spent with them, the less scared she got.

There was an axe by the front door next to a sign saying, *FOR EMERGENCY USE ONLY.* In the cellar, she saw the metal grate where water flowed in and out of house. A huge chain hung from the ceiling. She spotted a small shark fitted with a backpack and a flashing red light around its neck. It was carrying a headless Victorian squirrel in its mouth, releasing it and catching it, as though playing with a toy.

Reggie's first dive couldn't have lasted much more than ten minutes but it changed how she felt about everything. "That was amazing," she announced.

"I'm glad you enjoyed it."

"What was that on the small one's back?"

Professor Priestly looked at her with an expression she did not understand. "Reggie, I can't tell you everything, but if you're as clever as I think you are, you won't need me to."

Reggie returned home and found her mother in the kitchen holding the handle of a bread knife, the end of which was lodged in the kitchen tabletop.

"He's gone," she said. "Your father has left us."

"Where has he gone?"

"Does it matter?"

Reggie recognized this as a rhetorical question so said, "I've just been swimming with sharks."

"Maybe it's time you talked to someone."

"About what?"

"About these sharks."

"I could talk to you about them if you like," said Reggie, confused.

"Sometimes it helps to talk to someone ... objective. Someone independent about these sorts of things."

"Like a shark expert?"

"Yes, I suppose."

"That's what Professor Priestly is. He's a marine biologist."

Reggie was unsure why her mother threw her arms around her and cried into her hair, but she noticed that her mother said sorry twelve times, without ever explaining what she was apologizing for.

4.

Reggie discovered that home life was better with her dad gone, even if her mum did insist that she sat downstairs to watch television with her every evening. Reggie didn't want to refuse because she knew her mother felt lonely without all the arguing and shouting, but it meant she had to actually watch television rather than pretending. Her mother didn't seem to care what she was watching, so long as it filled the room with noise. It reminded Reggie of a camping holiday when they had all sat round a fire, staring at the flames, even though all it was doing was burning.

Reggie made no secret about her visits across the road to swim with sharks. She thought her mother was fine about it until she came home to find a smiling lady in a mint green cardigan on the sofa.

"Hello, Reggie," said the lady. "Your mother thought it might be a good idea if we had a chat."

"About what?"

"About the sharks."

"Are you a shark expert?" asked Reggie.

"No," replied the lady. "I'm a counselor. It's my job to listen to you."

"That sounds like an easy job," said Reggie. "Just listening."

"Do you find it easy to listen, Reggie?"

"Yes," said Reggie. "I'm listening to you now."

"Well, we can't both listen to each other. One of us needs to talk. Tell me about the sharks."

Reggie noticed the lady had a half drunk cup of tea and had left a Digestive biscuit untouched. "There are five sharks in the house across the road, except mating season will be soon so there will be more."

"How do sharks breathe in a house?"

"The house is full of water."

"How do you know?"

"I've been inside lots of times."

"What's it like inside . . . this house full of sharks?"

"It's quite like this house, except it's got all these weird objects in it and you can tell there was a fire there once."

"Fires, water, sharks. It sounds like a dangerous house. How does it feel when you're inside?"

Reggie had to think about this question. Professor Priestly had never once asked her about her feelings. He was more interested in the sharks than in her. He sometimes asked her what observations she had about the sharks but never her feelings about it. "At first it felt scary and I liked that feeling," she said.

"You enjoyed being scared?"

"Yes, I liked it because it made me forget everything else."

"Is that a nice feeling? Do you like forgetting everything else?"

"Yes. Isn't that why people do most things?"

"What kinds of things?"

"Read books, watch television, go to the movies, play sports."

"Yes, that's called escapism. Is that what the house full of sharks is? Is it a way of escaping from everything? Or do you feel as though the sharks are tearing you apart?"

"I . . . " Reggie noticed how the counselor looked at her over the top of her glasses and realized that it was one of those questions some adults asked that meant something else. "You think I'm making it up. You think it's not real."

"It's real if it feels real to you," said the green-cardigan lady. "Cold, unfriendly animals circling each other in a frightening environment, never knowing when someone is going to be at your throat. My guess is that you knew these feelings before you walked into a house of sharks."

"You can't walk into it. It's full of water. And it's not

143

imaginary. It's a house full of sharks." Reggie had noticed that when she felt angry her hands shook and her voice wavered, although she didn't notice this while she was in the middle of her anger. She didn't notice anything when she was like that.

Once the green-cardigan lady had gone and Reggie had calmed down, her mother sat down with her to watch television. While her mother stared at the screen, Reggie's mind wandered. She noticed that her dad's vinyl album collection had gone. She noticed that the clock on the wall had stopped. She noticed that her mother's nail varnish was chipped.

There was a detective show on television, in which a policeman wearing ordinary clothes had to piece together conveniently placed clues to solve a murder. It reminded her of what Professor Priestly had said about how scientists had to draw conclusions from the things they noticed. It was easy for the television detective to draw conclusions because he knew what the mystery was, whereas Reggie didn't know what she was supposed to know.

5.

Reggie had noticed how Professor Priestly usually spoke quietly on the phone, but when she next climbed down into the attic, he was shouting angrily. "No . . . no . . . no, you can't. You must reconsider . . . I . . . You can't. This is different . . . This isn't the last you will hear of this!"

He turned off the phone and looked at Reggie.

"What's wrong?"

"They're pulling my funding. Ravenscroft said my results were inconclusive. I told him I need more time but he won't listen."

"Is Ravenscroft the name of your boss?" asked Reggie.

"Yes."

Reggie was pleased with herself for inferring something but Professor Priestly didn't even notice. "I thought we shared a vision of creating a unique weapon."

"What weapon?"

"A division of trained sharks, armed with missiles."

"Sharks carrying missiles?"

"Sharks that are missiles," said Professor Priestly. "Exploiting their natural ability to follow electrical currents in order to target enemy submarines. It was a brilliant idea and it would have worked."

"But ... " Reggie felt her hands and voice begin to go. "The sharks are your family."

"No, I said they thought of me as family. They are my subjects. I have no emotional feelings about them one way or another. But I'll be damned if I'm going to sit back and let the military sell them off."

"What can you do?"

Professor Priestly picked up a torch and shone it into the hatch. "They have turned off the fresh water coming in. If the sharks remain here, they will soon stagnate and die." He picked up an oxygen tank and put it on his back. "I'll open the grate and flush the house."

"They'll end up in the sewer."

"Yes, but they'll stand more of a chance there than they have here."

"Can I come? I'd like to say goodbye."

"Sorry," he replied. "No time. Besides, once I flush the house with the grate open, the entire contents of the house will go down that plughole. The force would drag you down in a second."

"What about you?"

"I know what I'm doing."

He grabbed a harpoon, dropped into the hatch and splashed down into the house. Reggie paced as she waited. To calm her nerves, she looked around for things to notice so she could work out what they meant.

"Professor Priestly never takes his phone with him into the house," she said out loud. "My theory is that this is because it is not waterproof. The only way to open the grate into the sewer is to use the keys that are on the table. If the keys are still on the table then Professor Priestly cannot open the grate. My theory is that he must have forgotten to pick them up."

She waited for him to return.

He did not return.

"Professor Priestly has not come back for the keys. My theory is that . . . Come on, Reggie. Infer. Draw conclusions." She picked up the keys and looked down at the water. Something was disturbing it.

"What is it?" said Reggie. "What should I know? He doesn't have the keys. He does have a harpoon. He . . . My theory is that Professor Priestly . . . " And then she understood. "Professor Priestly has not gone to save the sharks. He has gone to kill them."

Reggie pulled on a wetsuit, grabbed the keys and torch, then jumped into the water. The sound of her own breathing filled her head as she swam down into the murky water. She swam past the mahogany-mounted cow bone into the hallway. A shark's face appeared in front of her. It was one of the females but her dead eyes were even deader than usual. The dead shark floated past, almost peacefully, until one of the other females appeared from the bathroom and took a bite out of its lifeless neck. Reggie swam on.

She felt sickened. She grabbed the bannister and pulled herself down the stairs. Dark blood spilled out of the lounge. Reggie had no idea if sharks made a noise when they were frightened but she felt as though she could hear their screams.

She swam down the cellar steps where she spotted the small shark with the harness on its back. Professor Priestly had betrayed them. She looked into the small shark's eyes, wondering if it understood what had happened to it or if it knew what was going to happen now. She swam down to the grate and fiddled with the key to open it. She swam up to the shark and tried to shoo him through the grate but he refused to go.

Reggie grabbed the flushing chain and tugged with all her might. The water swirled and she felt the pressure on her legs. Everything was being dragged out of the house. She held on with both hands but it was difficult. It felt as though she was being torn apart. Sharks, water and blood rushed past her as they shot out of the house. In amongst the bloody confusion, a hand grabbed her leg. Professor Priestly looked up at her, with wild desperation in his eyes. She had no idea what he would have said had he been able to speak. The largest shark was also desperately fighting the current. It closed its jaws on the professor's leg to save itself. Professor Priestly's expression shifted to that of pure terror before he released his grip and was gone. The last of the water rushed out and Reggie collapsed onto the floor, gasping and panting.

She pulled out her mouthpiece and shouted, "Professor!" but there was no reply.

Reggie stood up for the first time in the house, now fully drained of water. She picked up the headless squirrel and dropped it into the hole. Her limbs felt strangely heavy as she walked up the stairs for the first time but there was no way of reaching the attic, so she went back down, picked up the axe by the front door and hacked until her hands blistered and she could see daylight.

That evening she wrote three final entries in her book.

People notice when you come home in a wetsuit covered in blood.

People did not believe the house across the road was full of water and sharks but now they do believe it was full of water.

Noticing things isn't enough. You need to think about what they mean and act on them before it's too late.

The Art of Scaring

1.

"CAN WE GO trick or treating now?" asked the sad zombie.
Charlie felt bad. His son, Oscar, was five years old and
all he wanted to do was to enjoy Halloween. Instead he was
sitting on a pile of A4 paper in a cupboard, waiting for his dad
to finish work.

"We'll go in a minute," said Charlie. "I just need Daisy to
sign off this show."

Oscar, the sad zombie, didn't know about this meant. His
daddy was a television editor but he didn't make the kind of
television Oscar liked to watch.

"Is Daisy your boss?" he asked.

"No. She's my producer."

"Are you her boss?"

"It's not like that. We work together."

"Like Mummy and Joe?"

"No. Well, yes, except I don't live with Daisy. I only work with her."

"Where is she, then?"

"She's up in the office. This is the edit suite. It's where Daddy does his job. Do you like it?"

Oscar had no strong feelings about the room. It was on the ground floor so there was nothing to see out of the window, and even though it had three screens, not one of them was showing cartoons. "Why is it sweet?" he asked.

"It's not. Suite is spelled differently. It means . . . I don't know. I suppose it's another word for a room."

"Joe gives me sweets when I tidy my room," said Oscar.

"That's nice of him."

"Yes. So can we go trick or treating now?"

"Soon."

"What if the people run out of sweets?"

"I can buy you sweets."

"It's not really about sweets. I want to scare people and say trick or treat."

"There are lots of people up in the office. We can go up and scare them if you like."

"You can't do trick or treating in offices. You have to knock on doors."

Charlie let out a frustrated growl.

Oscar responded with one of his scariest zombie hisses.

Charlie did a scared whimper, which usually made Oscar laugh but not today. The door opened and Oscar pulled his feet in, tucking himself inside the cupboard. A lady he didn't know came into the room. She had brown hair and carried an exercise book like the ones Oscar had in school except hers was dark blue. She sat next to Charlie, facing the biggest screen. She did not notice the sad zombie in the cupboard. "Charlie, hi. So where are we with this, then?"

Charlie glanced at Oscar.

The sad zombie glared back.

"It's coming together nicely," said Charlie, "but, look, Daisy, could we view tomorrow? I can't really stay late tonight. My son –"

"I wish I couldn't stay late. What with these docs plus coverage of the big event to organize, I'll be lucky to get out by midnight."

Charlie knew that the longer he waited without mentioning the sad zombie in the cupboard, the harder it would be to bring it up. "As I say, it's Halloween and –"

"I don't really have time for this, Charlie. I've got to be in on this production meeting in a minute and this needs to be ready for a viewing with the exec tomorrow."

Oscar's daddy mouthed 'sorry' at him and hit the space bar on the keyboard. The biggest screen showed a man walking slowly and talking seriously in the way that people often did on television but not in real life.

"Jonathan Ravenscroft has had a remarkable career," said the man. "As a film producer, he was responsible for such controversial classics as *The Little Finger of Frankenstein*, *The Man with No Presence* and *The Unday of the Dead* . . . "

The screen showed black and white films with strange-looking people dressed up as old-fashioned vampires and unrealistic monsters.

"But his fiction pales in comparison to the horror of his work for the Planning Department at Larkin Mills Council."

"Stop there," said Daisy.

Charlie paused the program on the man's face.

"Strap him," said Daisy. "We need to know who's talking."

"OK. Hold on."

Oscar's dad typed something and made words appear on screen. He wrote *Professor Kyle Hasmi, Historian.*

"So what happens next?' asked Daisy.

"Interviews."

The show started again and cut to an old man in an armchair next to a roaring fire. According to the caption, this was *Sebastian Ravenscroft, Brother.*

"Yes . . . Jonathan was always extremely inventive. As children at play, I would come up with what I thought was a good idea, only to find that he had come up with fifteen better ones."

"Stop, stop, stop," cried Daisy.

The picture froze.

"Who is this?"

"It's his brother," replied Charlie.

"Yes, I know that. I can read. He's boring. Why should we care about any of this stuff?"

"It's background."

"Exactly. We need the foreground first. We can come back to this stuff. The show is called *The Man Who Made a Zombie Army.* It is not called the man who had a good imagination as a child."

Oscar recognized his dad's exasperated face. Apparently Daisy did not. "Carry on," she said.

"Maybe you should try watching the whole thing rather than interrupting every three –"

"No, I haven't got time," Daisy interrupted him. "Show me the good stuff now."

"By good stuff, you mean . . . "

"Death and destruction. War. Show me some of the war footage we spent all that money on."

Charlie moved the computer mouse and everything whizzed past until he stopped on a tank driving through a desert. It was the sort of thing that appeared on the news, where it looked horrible, rather than the sort in films, where war looked kind of fun.

"It was while serving in the army that Ravenscroft was taken prisoner for six agonizing months," said the presenter's voice. "He endured hardship, isolation and torture. His only escape from this bleak existence was a book of horror stories called *The Art of Scaring.*"

A book cover with the title appeared on screen.

"Blah blah blah," said Daisy.

Charlie paused the program. "You know, the show would be so much stronger if we had an interview with Ravenscroft himself."

"Well, we didn't get one, did we? And now it's too late." Daisy glanced at her watch. "I've got to go in a minute. This needs work."

"What work does it need?" Oscar wondered what would happen if he spoke to his teachers the way his dad was speaking to Daisy.

"Do you know how long most people give a TV show before switching over, Charlie?" demanded Daisy.

"No."

"Six seconds. Six seconds before your average channel hopper channel hops. The way this is shaping up, the only viewers left will be those who have fallen asleep before they got a chance to hit the remote control. I need to see the good stuff."

"But this background is vital to the narrative. It shows how

Ravenscroft used fictional horror to escape the real horrors of war, then went on to combine those two things."

"Fascinating." Oscar didn't know if Daisy's was a real yawn but it made him yawn too. "Just show me some zombies. Show me experiments and mad scientists. Show me the flesh of the story, Charlie. Show me the flesh."

Charlie moved the cursor and found the presenter standing in a shadowy tunnel and speaking in a whisper.

"It was when Ravenscroft's film career ended that he returned to Larkin Mills, and came up with the idea that would earn him the mantel The Man Who Would Have Made a Zombie Army."

"That's not right," said Daisy. "It's *The Man Who Made a Zombie Army.*"

"But he never succeeded," said Charlie.

"For crying out loud, the channel is screening four documentaries in the run up to the big event. The titles have already been listed: *The Doctor Who Stole His Patients' Health*, *The Woman Who Never Aged*, *The Mayor Who Sold Her Town* and *The Man Who Made a Zombie Army*. Cut out *Would Have.*"

Oscar was impressed at how fast his dad's fingers moved and how quickly he made it so the presenter said, "The man who ... made a zombie army."

"That's better," said Daisy. "You can cover that later. Carry on."

"Ravenscroft's film career was over but his horror career had only just begun," said the presenter. "He was about to come up with a way of turning war's largest by-product into its biggest resource."

The screen showed footage of soldiers being shot in slow motion along with the sound of machine gun fire. Oscar hugged his legs and pretended that he was watching a film. Slowly the image mixed to rows and rows of white crosses in a field. Charlie tried to move his chair to block Oscar's view of the screen, but Daisy nudged him back.

"This is excellent. Really good stuff," she said.

The presenter carried on. "Ravenscroft's idea was to reanimate the dead bodies and turn them into an army. One of the first people he went to with the idea was a doctor who also worked for the Planning Department, Doctor Finbar Good."

A man in a white coat, sitting in front of a human skeleton said, "Ravenscroft turned up at my office completely unannounced. He was all excited. Doctor Good, he said, war is a terribly wasteful thing, isn't it? All that human life. Yes, I replied, it is senseless. Except that wasn't what he meant, was it?"

"Hold on," said Daisy. "How did Ravenscroft end up in the Planning Department?"

"That's explained in the bit you didn't watch."

"Well, we'll need to hear all that, won't we?"

Oscar found it extremely annoying how they both kept talking over the program. He was trying to listen.

" ... weaponizing sharks, for which he ... "

"What was that?" said Daisy. "What's he talking about? Go back."

Charlie made everything go backwards, which looked really funny. This time they all listened to the presenter talking.

"During his time in the department, Ravenscroft was responsible for overseeing experiments into invisibility, the possibilities of extra-terrestrial landings, cloud-poisoning, and even the idea of weaponizing sharks, for which he gave marine biologist Professor Caspian Priestly permission to study his subjects in a specially designed suburban house. Extravagantly expensive and wildly ambitious experiments but to what end?"

"That shark thing sounds interesting. Have we got any more on that?" asked Daisy.

"Some of the interviewees mention it but there wasn't much time to leave it in."

"Good. We'll pitch it as a follow up show. *The Man Who Made a Shark Army.* Cut it out of this bit."

Daisy scribbled this down on her pad. Oscar couldn't see her handwriting but he could tell from the way she wrote that it was the messy kind.

"But this is the only take we have of this link," said Charlie. "It won't make sense if I cut out that bit."

"Make it make sense. Look, I don't have time to watch this now. It's clearly nowhere near ready. I've got a meeting in five minutes. Sort this out, Charlie. Start off with the zombies. Don't be afraid to make it scary. Really horror film scary, except even scarier because this is real. You can put all the background guff in afterwards."

"Sorry. I can't stay late tonight," said Charlie.

"But I told you, the exec is viewing it tomorrow."

"Tonight's Halloween. I promised my son we'd go trick or treating."

"Yes, but this has to be done." Oscar didn't think she was listening.

Charlie caught Oscar's eye. "My son is under the impression that trick or treating has to be done."

"He's a child. What does he know?"

"He knows when his father has promised him something."

Daisy placed a hand on Charlie's arm and spoke in a weird sort of little girl voice. "Please, Charlie-warlie. You know you're the only one who can do this. And Halloween. What is it, anyway? It's not exactly Christmas Eve. It's just a silly American import ... Please ... For me."

Charlie was no longer looking at his son. "Oh all right, I'll see what I can do in the next half hour, but I can't be longer than that."

"This meeting will take an hour," said Daisy. "I'll be back then. Thanks, Charlie. You're the best. We'll nail this thing. You've got the content. Don't be afraid to rely on the reconstruction zombie stuff. This whole thing needs to be three hundred per cent scarier."

She left the room.

Charlie swivelled round on his chair so that he was face to face with his son. "I'm sorry. This won't take long."

"Can we go trick or treating now?"

Hearing the question again, Charlie was unable to hide his frustration. "Oscar, you heard that entire conversation. This has to be done."

"Could Joe take me instead?"

"It would take me an hour to drive you to Mummy's. The ring road is hellish in rush hour."

"But you promised."

"I know, but now ... "

"Now, you're unpromising?"

"Oscar, I haven't got time for this. The sooner I get started, the sooner we can get out of here."

"Why does Daisy want it to scare people?"

"I don't know. I think she thinks people want to be scared."

"Did that man really make zombie soldiers?"

"No. He didn't succeed and they weren't really zombies. They would have been reanimated cor— Listen, Oscar, you're a bit young for all this."

"I like zombies … And I like sharks."

"I don't want to give you nightmares."

"You can't have nightmares about sharks, silly."

"Your mother told me that sometimes you wake up screaming."

"Not about sharks," said Oscar sulkily.

"What about then?"

Oscar's nightmares were always the same. In them he was dead, except he wasn't a zombie or a ghost or an angel. He was nothing. He couldn't see his hand or any part of his body and when he tried to talk he couldn't hear his voice. He screamed but no sound came out. It was a relief to wake up and find Mummy or Joe there. It was a relief to hear the sound of his own screams. He hadn't told anyone about the nightmare because he knew that they would say it was silly, but it wasn't because it was true. One day he really would be nothing.

"Can we go trick or treating now?"

"No, Oscar," yelled Charlie. "No, we cannot go trick or treating. I have to work. That's what grown-ups have to do."

Charlie hadn't meant to shout. He hated seeing Oscar cry. It was even worse when it was his fault. The sad zombie wept.

"Oscar, please."

Charlie reached out to comfort him but Oscar shrunk away from his touch.

"I just want to scare someone," said Oscar.

"Listen, Oscar, I've just had an idea. Do you want to hear my idea?" Oscar didn't respond but he stopped wailing. "Daisy wants this program to be scary. I can make it scary. Only, we'll make it really scary, then we'll play a trick on her."

"What kind of trick?"

"At the right moment, when she's all scared and tense, a real scary zombie will bang on the window. That's you, Oscar. If you want to scare someone then this will be the scariest thing ever. Come on, give us your best zombie hiss."

Oscar hissed.

"You can do better than that."

He hissed again, showing his teeth and widening his eyes.

Charlie recoiled in mock-fear and gave a thumbs up. "I bet she'll scream."

"Won't you get in trouble?"

"Who cares? I've been making shows like this since Daisy was in pigtails."

"She had a pig's tail?" asked Oscar.

"It's a ... It doesn't matter. What do you say? Shall we give her a Halloween to remember?"

"OK. Then, can we go trick or treating?"

"Yes, then we can go trick or treating."

Oscar watched his dad work for a bit then got bored so drew pictures of monsters on the paper he found in the cupboard. When Charlie had finished and Oscar had drawn twenty-three monsters, Charlie explained how he would signal Oscar by raising his hand.

"Then you'll bang on the window," he said.

"I'll bang on the window," said Oscar.

Charlie handed him the car keys. "Then run straight to the car so you don't get spotted."

"Run to the car."

Charlie left Oscar outside and went back to the suite, where he found Daisy sitting waiting for him.

"Oh, hi, Daisy. Sorry. I just nipped out to the toilet."

"So, where are we with this, Charlie?" asked Daisy.

"I did what you asked," he replied.

"Let's see it, then."

Charlie pressed play. On the screen, a pair of feet in tattered shoes staggered through dark puddles. A low, pained moan joined the sound of footsteps.

"What is the biggest by-product of war?" asked a disembodied voice. "Death. No war has ever been fought that did not produce legions of dead bodies. Most consider this a waste, a terrible waste. One man considered them a resource. That was Jonathan Ravenscroft ... The Man Who Made a Zombie Army."

The shot moved up to reveal loose-fitting skin falling off the bones of the solitary zombie.

"It's the stuff of nightmares," said another voice. "Reanimating dead bodies and turning them into an indestructible army."

The presenter spoke again. "Ravenscroft's idea was to capture enough enemy corpses to create an army, in order for the enemy to fight their own dead. In war one must try to depersonalize the enemy, but what if you're pointing a gun at the dead body of your own brother or your best friend? It's a kind of genius."

A low drone grew louder and louder as more stumbling zombies moved closer. The sound of a gunshot accompanied a sudden lurch forward. The screen turned dark red before fading to black.

Charlie paused the show and gave the signal. The wind had picked up outside and there was something walking past on hooves.

Clip clop, pause ...

Clip clop, pause ...

But still there was no bang on the window.

Charlie gave the signal again. *Come on, Oscar*, he thought,

It's got to be now.

When it came, the bang on the window was so loud it even made Charlie jump.

Daisy screamed and leapt out of her seat.

Two red raw hands shook the window pane. Fingernails dragged down the glass. Daisy ran from the room, beside herself with terror. Charlie leaned back on his chair, clapped his hands and gave the thumbs up. "Well done. Brilliant. Nice one, Oscar."

He noticed that Daisy had left her exercise book. He scribbled the words, *Scary enough for you?* then left. He chuckled all the way back to the car where he found Oscar in the passenger seat with his seatbelt on.

"Ha. That was priceless. You should have seen her face. It was perfect timing. You must have been watching outside, were you? And the fingernails too. So sinister. Superb. It serves her right. That's a taste of her own medicine."

Oscar swung his legs. "Sorry, Daddy."

"Sorry about what? You did great."

"I came to sit here because I was cold. I forgot to go back and scare the lady."

"You ... What?"

"Sorry, Daddy."

Charlie could tell from his son's face he was telling the truth.

"But then ... " He looked out of the window. "Then who was that?"

It was dark outside the car, and Charlie couldn't see who was out there but he heard that sound again.

Clip clop, pause ...

Clip clop, pause ...

"Can we go trick or treating now?" asked Oscar.

Madam Letrec's World of Wax

1.

AFTER ONLY TWO WEEKS as a Dodgem Runner I left the steam fair altogether and went to live at the orphanage. Ever since tasting Mr. Morricone's ice cream, a creeping suspicion had been growing inside me that there was more to life than the thrill of cheating death. Anyone who left the fair had to pay exit-tax to the Fair Commandant, which is why I took the job at Madam Letrec's World of Wax.

While most waxwork museums boasted exact replicas of famous faces, Madam Letrec's housed a collection of obscure local dignitaries, forgotten historical figures and rough approximations of every mayor Larkin Mills had ever had.

The current in a long line of Madam Letrecs ran the museum from her office on the top floor of the building and refused to allow any modernization. Not that we cared. It was only a temporary job to most of us. Most of us only saw her once a day when she ventured downstairs at the closing time to collect the takings from the gift shop. The daily running of the museum was entrusted to the duty manager, a greasy-haired manboy in his early twenties with a failed attempt at a moustache on his upper lip. I took an instant dislike to him and he to me. Trope relished the morning's chastizings, during which we all had to stand in a line, while he walked in front of us, picking on people to tell off.

"Ross." I hated the way he hissed my name. "Ross, Ross, Ross . . . " He shook his head. "Remind me what duty you were on yesterday?"

"Hand checking," I said.

"Ah yes." He looked at his clipboard. "The vital role of standing by the sinks in the toilets to ensure everyone washes their hands properly." I couldn't tell if he was being sarcastic. He smirked to himself and checked his notes. "And yet I am told that no less than eight visitors did not use soap and instead opted for a cursory hand-wet and shake."

"There was a coach party," I said. "They all came in at once."

"I'm not interested in excuses," said Trope. "You're in Local Maniacs through the Ages today. I trust you can handle that." He moved on before I could respond. "Now, Seraphina . . . "

"Park."

He looked at his notes, then back at the girl. "Park, remind me of the correct way to greet visitors to the museum."

"Hello. Welcome to Madam Letrec's World of Wax, the world's oldest waxwork museum."

"Oh, you do know it," said Trope. "Next time you're on entrance duty, please try to remember it. You'll be in Maniacs too today." He took a step back to address us all. "Madam Letrec has asked me specially to remind you that you must behave in accordance with the rules of the museum." He read from his notes to ensure he got the exact wording. "*This museum has been open every single day for over a hundred years. Come rain or shine, winter, spring, summer or autumn, we are a constant reminder of this town's past. You are here to maintain our procedures. That means getting your words right, knowing where everything is, and being helpful and polite to our visitors.*" He folded the piece of paper and said, "Now, all of you to your positions, please, and remember: this may be a temporary job for you but, while you are Madam Letrec's employees, you are her representatives on Earth."

We filed out and I found myself walking beside Park.

"Her representative in hell more like," I said.

"No one's forcing you to work here," she replied.

"No, but I need the money. I'm saving up."

"What for?"

"You'll laugh."

"I promise not to."

"I want to set up an ice cream business."

"Why's that funny?"

"Because I don't know the first thing about ice cream."

"What's to know? It's cold and it tastes good. Besides, Morricone could do with some competition. Have you seen the queues he gets?"

"That's because there's nothing to do in this town. It beats me why people visit this museum."

"I know. I mean, look at this one." I stopped by a tall man in a smart suit. "*Jonathan Ravenscroft,*" I read out. "Who even is that?"

"He's that guy who tried to create a zombie army. He should

be in the maniac room."

"It doesn't say any of that here," I said.

"Yeah, well that's what this place is like. There are loads of interesting people here but, unless you know the stories about them, there's nothing to tell you what they really did. Take this one." At the bottom of the stairs was a man in a toga. "The plaque only says *Roman*, but this is Larkin, the soothsayer who gave the town its name. You see the two lumps on top of his head? The Romans believed they were the fingerprints of the gods."

"How do you know all this?"

"My dad wrote a story about him."

"What does your dad do?"

"He was an archaeologist but he's dead now. I'm saving for his funeral."

"I'm sorry."

"Don't be. It's what he wanted."

I didn't know how to respond to this so I changed the subject. "What's it like, working in Maniacs?"

"It's all right. Boring more than anything else."

"It can't be worse than watching people wash their hands," I said.

"Hand checking is one of the better jobs," she replied. "Last week I was in the remolding room. That's where they melt down the models that have lost their form or ones that they don't want any more. They melt them down and remold them. It's really hot and the wax gets all over your skin. You have to scrape it off with a spoon. Have you done the night shift yet?"

"No. What's that like?"

"Creepy but you get paid time-and-a-half after the doors close so I do it as often as I can."

"How late do you have to stay?"

"A security guard takes over at eleven. All the main lights go off at seven and you're stuck here for four hours with all these weird waxy faces staring at you."

"Back at the steam fair, we used to say that the exhibits came to life at night." I looked up the statue of a brutish man, labelled as, *Candle, Larkin Mills' First Mayor.*

"I think Letrec started that rumor to hide the truth," said Park.

"What truth?"

"About what she keeps in the attic."

"I didn't know there was an attic."

"Yep. There's a hatch above her desk in her office. I saw it once."

"Why do you think there's something in the attic?"

"Because late at night, when there's no one around, you can hear movement."

2.

I liked Park. She was interesting and she didn't seem to mind me hanging around with her all the time. She knew loads of stuff about historical figures. If she had been a tour guide they would have doubled the numbers of visitors overnight. She told me she lived in Milkwell's Funeral Guest House but that she would be moving out after her father's funeral.

When Trope asked for volunteers for the nightshift we both put our hands up and, since we were the only ones, Trope said, "All right, Ross and Park will work late tonight." He jotted this down. "Now, Madam Letrec is very concerned about the state of everyone's uniforms. Last week, she spotted three of you wearing non-regulation socks. From now on, the morning chastisings will also involve a full uniform inspection. If any of you are not up to scratch you will be sent home."

I spent the morning on crutch duty, which involved propping up a one-legged waxwork in the Good Old Days room. After lunch, I was on bin duty, which was a terrible job, except that it was with Park again. We had to empty every bin in the museum, then carry the bags down to the basement and drop them into the incinerator. The smell was awful. A bag had just split and we were picking up all the discarded drinks cups and food containers when I noticed a dumb waiter in one of the walls.

"What's that?" I asked.

"That's the poo lift," replied Park. "Don't let *that* bag split whatever you do."

I went to pick up the black bin bag inside and instantly understood what she meant. It reeked like dirty nappies, rotting food and unflushed toilets.

I quickly carried it to the shoot that led to the incinerator.

"Where does it come from?" I asked.

"One of the toilets, I suppose."

"How can it? I mean, we have to empty all the nappy bins in the toilets, don't we?"

"That, Ross, is a good point. Where does it come from? I've never thought of that. This wall runs up the middle of the building," said Park. "If we follow it up, it should be easy enough to find another opening. Come on, let's go look. We've got more collecting to do, anyway."

I followed her out. We picked up rubbish as we went up through the building but failed to find another little door for the dumb waiter. We checked all three floors but found nothing.

"Must be the top floor," I said.

Employees weren't supposed to use the lift so we took the stairs up to the corridor with Madam Letrec's office. There was no opening. Neither of us wanted to get caught creeping around the top floor so we headed back down.

"You know what this means," said Park, a tinge of excitement in her voice. "It must come from the attic. I told you. Something is up there."

Once we had emptied every bin in the museum we heard the bell signalling the end of the day, so we went to the entrance hall to begin the late shift.

"Do your parents know you're staying late?" asked Park.

"Parents?" said Trope. "Hasn't he told you? Ross lives in the Institute for Parentally Impoverished but Talented Youngsters. Don't you?"

"Yes." I hated Trope with every fiber of my body.

"Wow. What talent do you have?" asked Park. "I don't. They just call it that because they didn't want to say orphanage."

"Yes, the council said the word orphanage encouraged people to feel sorry for the residents. The only problem is that now the sign spells *I PITY* outside," said Trope. "I pity those poor orphans." He sniggered.

Park ignored him. She smiled kindly at me. "We can walk home together if you like."

Once Trope finished ticking everyone off his exit list, he turned back to us. "Park, you know the drill. Double check all the rooms are clear then lock the doors behind you. Don't touch anything and do not speak to Madam Letrec."

"Are these the late shift workers?" Madam Letrec stood in the doorway of the gift shop, clutching a bag of money. Her black hair was pulled up away from her milk-white face. Her skin was as tight and unblemished as that of a young woman, but her eyes revealed a wealth of experience. She wore black lace gloves, but I spotted thick veins protruding from the backs of her hands. It was the first time I had heard her voice, which was as ageless and unreadable as her face. Trope looked panicked by her sudden appearance.

"Yes ma'am. That's right. Ross and Park."

"What kind of name is Park?" asked Madam Letrec.

"My parents let me name myself after my first word," said Park.

"Well, Park and Ross," said Madam Letrec, pointedly, "stay off the third floor tonight. I am working late and do not want to be disturbed. Do you understand?"

We both nodded and Madam Letrec pressed the lift button. The door pinged as it opened and she stepped inside.

"I'll see you both tomorrow," said Trope. He turned off the lights and closed the door behind him. Park turned on her torch and placed it under her chin. "Scared yet?"

I tried to laugh it off but I was a little spooked. With the weird old waxworks casting long shadows in the low light, it was too easy to imagine their eyes watching us.

Once all the doors were locked, Park said, "So what about it?"

"What about what?"

"The top floor. You can hear the noises from above."

"You heard what she said."

"She won't come out of her office. She never does. Come on. Unless you're too scared . . . "

I didn't want to admit that I was, so I followed her up the stairs to the very top corridor where the only light was the white line around the edges of Madam Letrec's office door. Park pointed at the ceiling. I listened but I couldn't hear a thing over the blood pounding in my ears.

The office door opened and Park stepped back into the stairwell. She was standing on my toe but I stayed silent.

Madam Letrec said, "Ah, there you are."

Park and I looked at each other, thinking we had been caught.

"You look as youthful as ever," said a man's voice. "How's business?"

We peered around the corner and saw the speaker standing at the other end of the corridor. Madam Letrec had pushed the door wide open so the light from the office spilled out into the corridor. The man wore a deerstalker with two old-fashioned car horns sticking out of the top that kept his features hidden under its shadow.

"The museum is as good as you could reasonably expect. There's so much to compete with these days. So many other things one can do with one's time other than admiring wax effigies of the past."

"One day I should ask you to cast me."

"Some people are not so easily captured in wax," said Madam Letrec.

"What do you suggest?"

"For you, ice."

"Very funny. What do you want?"

"I'm starting up the club again," said Madam Letrec.

The man stepped forward so we could see his dark eyes, alive with excitement. A wicked smile revealed a set of dazzling white teeth. "Is that wise?" he said.

"Exclusive membership as before, vetted to ensure discretion.

171

Each will pay high premiums for the privilege, of course."

"Why are you telling me?"

"My collection is incomplete and I need you to complete it."

"Why should I? All I ever do is help people. Who ever helps me?"

"I can help you."

"How?" he demanded.

"Reconciliation?"

The man considered this. "It's too late for that."

"It's never too late."

"I don't think he's even here any more."

"He's here. He made himself invisible to us but I know a man who knows exactly where to find him."

The stranger shook his head. "I will not go back to him on bended knees."

"It will be different this time. Equal footing. Reconciliation on your terms."

The man considered this. "There would have to be sacrifices. You know what he's like."

"You can sort that out amongst yourselves. I'm offering to help you find him ... if you help me."

"What would you want in exchange?"

"That which you once created."

"Oh, him. You want to put him up there with those other unfortunate souls and exhibit him like an animal in a zoo, do you?"

"Do this and I will tell you how to find your old master."

"I suppose it would be good to catch up with him. It's been a long time."

"So we have a deal?"

"We have a deal." The man offered his hand.

Madam Letrec shook it and said, "The undertaker, Mr. Milkwell. He has remained loyal all this time. He knows where to find him."

"He won't talk to me."

"You still have employees, don't you?"

"More than ever."

"Send one of those. Now, I have fulfilled my side of the deal."

"I'll make the delivery on Saturday."

The man turned and walked back down along the corridor and Madam Letrec disappeared into her office. Under the blanket of darkness, Park and I headed back down the stairs.

"What was that all about?" I asked.

"I don't know," she replied. "But we were blocking the only way up to that the corridor. However that man got in, it wasn't through the door."

3.

On the walk home, there was a point when our hands swung so close that mine brushed the back of Park's. I pulled it away, embarrassed. "I wonder who it is they were talking about. Who is it Mr. Milkwell knows how to find?" I said.

"I don't know, but there's definitely something strange about him and his son. I always get the feeling Mr. Milkwell has a murky past. I can't wait to get out of that place."

"You mean after your father's funeral?"

"Yes."

We stopped outside the funeral guest house. A downstairs curtain twitched and I caught a glimpse of someone watching us.

"Isn't it creepy sharing the home with all those dead people?"

I asked, trying to find a way of keeping her from leaving.

"No creepier than sharing a home with all those untalented orphans, I'd imagine."

I would have come up with a follow-up question but she threw me off by kissing me on the cheek and walking away. I didn't know what the kiss meant but I took it as a good sign when, the next morning, Park took a place next to me for the daily chastisings.

"Please remember that customers must always exit the museum through the gift shop," said Trope. "One of you let a man out through the main entrance yesterday."

"But he was having a heart attack," protested a mousy-haired girl with a face like a porcelain doll. "There was an ambulance outside."

"No exceptions. Another thing regarding the gift shop. Please will you all remember to try to sell the industrial-sized paperweights in particular. They've got ten per cent off this week."

"But they're so heavy," said a boy who was either called Gerard or Gerald. I was never sure which. "We haven't got bags strong enough to hold them."

"This isn't a discussion," said Trope angrily. "Madam Letrec is very concerned about falling standards. This museum has been in her family for a long time. You must maintain the high standards that our visitors have come to expect. Now, before I assign today's duties, Madam Letrec has asked me to inform you that the museum will be closed tomorrow."

"Tomorrow's Saturday," said Park. "And we're right in the middle of steam fair season. It's one of the busiest times of the year. Why would she close the museum?"

"I'm sorry? Is your name Madam Letrec?" said Trope. "No,

it's not, in which case it's none of your business. You'll all be required to take one of your holiday days tomorrow and come back to work on Sunday."

We all grumbled about this but there wasn't an opportunity to talk about it with Park until lunchtime, when we were sat in the spare limbs room. The contracts we signed when we started included a whole bunch of clauses about eating. We were only allowed to eat in the designated eating areas, out of sight of the customers. We were not allowed to be seen eating in uniform. We were permitted to consume liquids during the day providing they were colorless and did not contain sugar. One of the clauses simply read, *Pies are unacceptable.* None of us knew whether that was a statement of opinion or if we were not allowed to eat pies while working at the museum. Just in case, we all avoided pies.

"So what do you think?" said Park. "What's she up to?"

"Who?"

"Letrec. You heard her last night. She's opening up a secret club and she's shutting the museum for the first time in a hundred years. What's she doing? What was she asking that man to get her?"

"A waxwork, I suppose."

"Don't be silly." Park picked up a wax arm and scratched her ear with it, imitating an orangutan.

I laughed.

"This club she's setting up is obviously something people want to see."

"Like what?"

"I don't know," admitted Park, "but my dad once told me a story about Madam Letrec."

"You mean how she isn't an ancestor of the original Madam

Letrec? How she is the original Madam Letrec and is centuries old?" I said.

"How do you know?"

"My dad told me the same story. He said that years ago she did a deal with the devil to keep her looking young. It's silly. Just the sort of stuff adults tell kids."

Park scratched the top of my head with the disembodied wax hand. "This is Larkin Mills, Ross. Anything is possible."

"What do you mean? Larkin Mills is like any other town."

She shook her head. "No, it's not. I've been to other towns. This one is different. My dad says . . . said that something happened here years ago. There were two visitors. Visitors from another world."

"Like aliens?" I couldn't help laughing.

"Yes. They were at war before they arrived and they brought that war to Earth. We have been fighting their battles ever since."

"What battles? What war?"

"Good and evil . . . Right and wrong . . . God and the devil."

"Oh, so it's one of those stories," I said.

"What do you mean by that?" she replied.

"It's made up."

"All stories are made up. Only some are made up of facts and some are made up of lies. I don't *know* which this one is but I *think* it's a bit of both."

"So what happened to the visitors? I mean, in the end."

"They're immortal. I don't think there is an end."

"So the guy we saw talking to Madam Letrec was the devil?"

"He did have horns."

"Car horns," I said doubtfully. "And what? He's looking for God?"

"I suppose."

"Why here? Why Larkin Mills?"

"I don't know but, whatever the truth, we need to find out what she's getting delivered."

4.

We agreed to meet by *The Big Heart* at nine the next morning. I was a couple of minutes early and Park was a few minutes late so I sat listening to a girl playing an oboe, feeling bad that I didn't have any money to throw into her case.

When Park arrived, we didn't have to wait long until a large white truck pulled up outside the museum. It did a three-point turn and reversed towards the main door.

I followed Park across the road. As we reached the van, there were three traffic wardens circling it, papering the windscreen with parking fines. I couldn't tell if there was a driver in the cabin. We went round the back where red velvet curtains hung from the back of the van to the museum door, hiding whatever was being unloaded. Park dropped to her knees and tried to look under but it was firmly attached to the ground.

"Ross, have you got a knife?" she asked. "We could cut it."

"No," I said. I was grateful I didn't. It was bad enough that we were carrying out an illegal junior investigation without adding criminal damage to our list of crimes.

We heard the van doors open and the sound of metal scraping against metal.

"They're lowering the ramp," whispered Park.

I could hear the oboe playing a fast, exciting piece of music. It was really good but it was putting me on edge. On the other side of the curtain we heard hooves coming down the ramp.

Clip clop pause . . .

Clip clop pause . . .

"Two feet," mouthed Park, holding up her fingers.

I couldn't think of an animal with hooves that walked on two feet. It drew level with us, breathing hard.

The museum door opened and Madam Letrec gasped. "Magnificent. I'm so delighted you could join us. Please, come this way."

The creature responded, not with words but with an exhalation of breath.

"Follow me."

Clip clop pause . . .

Clip clop pause . . .

"This is too interesting," said Park. "We've got to find a way inside."

"Break into the museum on the only day it's ever been closed when we've been told to stay away? Are you mad?"

"You're right. It's too risky. Tomorrow we'll volunteer for rubbish duty.

"Why would we do that?"

"Those stinking buckets are coming from the attic. That's where we need to go."

"How?"

"In the dumb waiter."

"The poo lift?" I exclaimed.

"Dad once told me that you have to dig through layers of filth to find the smallest piece of gold."

I don't know why I ever questioned Park. I would have followed her anywhere.

The next day, when the poo lift arrived, the smell of the bag was even worse than usual. I carried it to the incinerator and dropped it in. When I turned around, I saw Park had already crammed herself inside. I paused. Not because of the insanity of what we were about to do but because when I climbed in I would be pressed up against her.

"Quickly," she said, "before it moves."

I squeezed in and felt her leg against my arm.

"Are you ready?" she said.

"No," I replied.

The dumb waiter rattled and moved up through the building. It was mostly dark, with occasional glimpses of light through cracks in the wall. The lift took us up past the main display room, the notable council workers and famous maniacs then up to the top floor and beyond. When it stopped, Park pushed a flap open and climbed out. The floorboards squeaked. Thin beams of daylight shone through the dirty windows in the sloping roof, highlighting the swirling dust. Three shapes moved in the shadows.

"Flesh," hissed a voice.

"Human fleshhhh," said another.

Park took my hand. We backed away but I could hear the dumb waiter trundling down through the building. There was no way out. Neither of us fancied plunging straight into the shaft.

"My name is Park. This is Ross." Park's voice sounded braver than her shaking hand felt.

"Young flesh from below," said the voice.

"Human fleshhh," hissed the other.

"Who are you? Do you live up here?" asked Park.

"We exist up here. It is no life." The speaker stepped into the light and I could see a horribly misshapen head, with a large bulbous protrusion from its temple.

"Does she keep you locked up here?" asked Park.

179

"We are her prisoners," said the man. In spite of the nightmarish sight of his head, I found myself feeling sorry for him.

"The fleshhh will help usss," said the other voice.

The voice belonged to something that was dragging itself across the floorboards. It looked as though there was a huge tail where there should have been a pair of legs. Half man, half slug.

"What are you?" I said.

"Ross," scolded Park. "They are prisoners. Can't you see?"

"No, the boy flesh is right," said the misshapen head. "Once we were human. Now, we are little more than forgotten exhibits."

"Freaksss," whispered the slug-bodied man. "Experiments made by humans more interested in progress than kindness. Two of us are products of Doctor Good's redistribution of health."

"What about him?" I pointed to the third silent figure.

He stepped into the light and I saw the reason for his silence. The figure's head was perfectly bald. He had dark eyes and a small stubby nose, but no mouth. I looked away in revulsion.

"One of Ravenscroft's rejectsssss. Letrec took us in when they threw us out. This attic is our prison. You must help us escape it." The poor man stepped forward and grasped our hands. His flesh felt soft and damp and I could see that he had long blackened nails.

"It's not right. People don't treat other people like this any more," said Park.

"This new one is different," said the misshapen head.

I could hear the rattle of the dumb waiter returning and the clip-clop approach of a two-legged hooved animal across the wooden floor of the attic.

Clip clop, pause . . .

"Pleasssse," said the slug-man.

"We'll call the police," said Park.

"No. The police are her friends. They will not help."

"The hatchsh," said the slug man, pointing to the door in the floor. "The hatchsh can only be opened from below."

The dumb-waiter clicked into place. "Come on," I said. "We must go."

Clip clop, pause . . .

Clip clop, pause . . .

I dragged Park into the dumb waiter as the fourth figure shifted in the shadows. I saw no face but I did see its raw red hands and a pair of curled horns on its head. The poo lift carried us away, down to safety.

"You know, this is precisely why junior investigations are against the law in Larkin Mills," I said.

"We have to open the hatch," said Park. "We must help them escape."

"Why? It's got nothing to do with us?"

"Yes it has. We've seen them with our own eyes. We're the only ones who can put this right."

"But what about the other one?" I said. "Even they're scared of that thing with hooves."

"Only because it's new," she said. "I bet that whatever that poor creature is, he is just as scared as they are. We need to help them get out. We'll do it tonight. When Madam Letrec goes down to pick up the till money, we'll sneak in and unlock the attic door."

5.

At lunchtime, Park asked Trope if we could swap with whoever was doing the night shift.

"Need the money for Daddy's funeral, do you?" he said. "Well, you'll have to wait. There's no nightshift this evening."

"No nightshift?" said Park. "Why?"

"It's none of your business is why."

Once he had gone, Park turned to me. "I'll bet it's opening tonight. The freak club. We'll have to open the hatch at the end of the day instead."

"It's impossible. We'll be leaving at the same time that she'll be coming down."

"It's possible," she said. "If I go up and wait on the top floor, then as soon as she leaves the office I can slip in, open that hatch and get out before she gets back."

"But we'll only have five minutes to get out before we're locked in for the night."

"It's tight but possible. Now, let's think it through."

By the end of the day we had come up with a plan. We would get ourselves checked off Trope's exit list then Park would go to the toilet and I would say I had left something behind. Park would take the stairs to the top floor and enter the office as soon as Madam Letrec left to pick up the takings. I would be on watch downstairs and run up to warn Park as soon as I saw Madam call the lift.

My heart was racing when I told Trope that I had left my bag in the locker but he was too busy ticking names off his exit list to care about me. As Park had guessed, once our names were ticked off, as far as Trope was concerned his job was done. I hid behind a statue of a Roman commander called Clodius

Albinus, who was described as *Conqueror and Founder of Larkin Mills*. He looked so similar to the soothsayer that I wondered if the same mold had been used.

I heard the lift door open and saw Madam Letrec appear. However, instead of going into the shop she walked over to Trope. "Is everyone out?"

He checked his list. "Yes, all accounted for, ma'am."

"Excellent. Then good night, Trope. I'll see you tomorrow."

Madam Letrec locked the door behind him. This didn't worry me. Our plan was to leave through the museum entrance. She checked her appearance in the mirror at the bottom of the stairs. She was as pale as a ghost, but certainly did not look over a hundred years old. There was a knock on the door. Madam Letrec opened the main entrance.

"Mayor Kendall, Doctor Good, Mr. Ravenscroft, how good of you to be so prompt. Do come in," said Madam Letrec.

I recognized the two men from their waxwork effigies, but Mayor Kendall's face was well known in Larkin Mills. She had been in charge of the town for over thirty years and was often on the news announcing a new council ruling or making a speech about something or other.

"Madam Letrec," she said, wrinkling her nose and offering her hand. "You look well. You must let me know your secret one day."

"I'll take it to the grave with me," Madam Letrec responded with a polite smile.

"I hope you don't mind that I have packed a healthy amount of cynicism with regards to this club of yours," said Doctor Good.

"Indeed," said Mr. Ravenscroft. "After all, we were the ones who sold you most of these freaks."

"Whereas I would like to know how much this will cost?" said the mayor.

"Tonight there is no charge," said Madam Letrec. "I am confident that you will be back for further viewings and that you will want your friends to witness what you have witnessed."

"A dusty attic full of deformed freaks?" said Mr. Ravenscroft.

"It was popular enough back then," said Mayor Kendall. "But there is so much to compete with these days. The things they put on television are quite extraordinary."

"Yes, things were so much simpler back in the good old days," said Doctor Good.

"We are not here to reminisce," said Madam Letrec. "In this town, so much is possible. We four all know this to be the case. Tonight I will present you with the truth, that heaven and hell exist – not as constructs of our imaginations, but as real places populated by real creatures. Tonight I will show you a beast that was not born but forged out fire and bile."

"His demon?" whispered Mr. Ravenscroft.

"It's a myth," said Doctor Good.

"It is no myth," replied Madam Letrec. "My other freaks were created by men eager to challenge the laws of this world." She looked at Mr. Ravenscroft and Doctor Good. "But the centerpiece of my collection was created by a hand so ambitious that it sought to overthrow an omnipotent being. It is the embodiment of hope. This demon is the birth of rebellion."

"Is it dangerous?" asked Doctor Good.

"His keeper has given me handling instructions. So long as he remains in that attic, we have nothing to –"

Madam Letrec's words were cut short by a loud bang from above. "I'm sorry," she said. "I'd better check that."

She hit the lift button. I needed to warn Park. I turned and ran up the stairs. I had made it up one flight when I collided with her coming the other way.

"Run," she said.

Park looked terrified.

"Run!" she repeated.

There was another bang from above. Heavy footsteps thundered. There were crashes as objects were knocked over. Footsteps and thuds. The sound of the lift opening. We stepped out of the stairwell and I saw the light above the lift showing that it had reached the top floor. Park ran to the entrance and held the door open.

"Come on," she urged.

I heard the ping of the lift door opening. My feet were rooted to the spot.

Then we heard the screams.

I will never forget those screams.

When they stopped, all that remained was the sound of hooved feet.

Clip clop, pause …
Clip clop, pause …

Five Hundred Ways to Say Dead

1.

GONE TO SLEEP, at rest, at peace, deceased, departed, bowed out, taken a final sip of the good stuff, handed in your notice, taken the overnight train to Penzance, stepped out with the ragged dancer." Mr. Milkwell wagged his finger at his son. "There are over –"

"– five hundred ways to say dead. Yes, I know," said Campbell. "You've told me enough times."

"Obviously not enough for it to sink into all that cotton wool you keep between the ears, though, is it?"

"I don't have cotton wool between my ears. Besides, it was only Mr. Garner."

"It doesn't matter whether it's to the coffin maker, the flower arranger or the gravedigger, a good undertaker never says the D-word. You never know who might be listening. You never know who might take offence."

"But surely this funeral is different. It's all over the television and the radio. The local paper is giving away free parking spaces and front row seats for the big day. Everyone is talking about it. What difference does it make it if I say dead?"

"It is true that this *event*," corrected Mr. Milkwell, "is the biggest in the history of Larkin Mills. Four well-known, high-ranking members of this community met an unfortunate end on the same night. It's got it all: celebrity, glamour, drama. This is the big one." Mr. Milkwell slammed his hands down on the reception desk as he finished his speech, then, realizing he had got carried away, adjusted his tie and casually examined his fingernails. "So what did Mr. Garner have to say about the coffins?"

"He said he has four extremely ostentatious requests for four specially tailored coffins and has had to employ more staff to make the deadline ... "

"A-hem." Mr. Milkwell cleared his throat pointedly.

"What?" asked Campbell.

"The what-line?"

Campbell sighed. "He said he's had to employ more staff to make it in time. He said this will cost, and affect the quote he gave."

"No matter. I believe the right phrase, with regards to this Thursday's big event, is that money is no object. This is the one that every undertaker dreams of. An event like this is our moment to shine. The dignity which we bring to Thursday's proceedings will go down in history. Have I ever told you about your great grandfather?"

"How he was a pallbearer for Queen Victoria and how he wasn't even paid for it? That he did it for the love of funerals?

No, you've never mentioned it."

"I'll thank you for less of your cheek." Mr. Milkwell took a swipe at Campbell's ear but his son dodged. "I blame that girl, with all her ideas, leading you astray."

"Park's gone now," said Campbell, hoping his eyes wouldn't betray his feelings about that.

"Good. She was a bad influence."

"There was another message," said Campbell. "A salesman called." He handed his father the note with a telephone number written under a question mark.

"What was he selling?"

"Questions."

"Sounds like another journalist sniffing around for dirt."

"I don't think so." Campbell had learned to spot journalists over the last couple of weeks. "He sounded too knowing to be a journalist."

"Knowing?" said Mr. Milkwell. "What did he know?"

"I don't know." Campbell shrugged.

"Did he say what questions he was selling?"

"He said we'd have to pay up front."

"Must have been a prank caller. Who in their right mind would buy a question without knowing what it was? An answer, perhaps. But a question? It's nonsense." Mr. Milkwell screwed up the piece of paper and threw it into a bin under the desk. "Now, we have much to do."

"But it's the qualifiers this evening."

"There'll be plenty enough time for sport in the future. This is a once in a lifetime opportunity to shine. I need you to dye the ostrich feathers for Madam Letrec's horses. Now, was there anything else?"

"That TV woman called."

"Daisy?" Mr. Milkwell smoothed down his hair with his palm.

"Yes, she said the event is going to go out live now. Also, they've decided on a name. It's going to be called *The Funeral*. She said it wasn't like anyone didn't know whose funeral it was."

"Well, she knows her business. She told me that they're expecting unprecedented viewing figures. The documentaries about the four dearly departed have rated very well."

"Four documentaries," exclaimed Campbell. "And not one investigating the death itself."

"Oh, please. Not this again," said Mr. Milkwell. "Wild animals escaping zoos and attacking people is hardly unheard of."

"What animal? What zoo?"

"As undertakers, we do not question how our clients passed away. The only question we should ask is what we can do to assist with the arrangements."

2.

As the day of the funeral approached, Campbell became well accustomed to all the extra attention. It was not uncommon for people to follow him home. He had just passed the pet gymnasium when he realized there was someone in the shadows. He turned around to see a man wearing glasses and a grey suit, and holding a black briefcase.

"What do you want?" demanded Campbell.

"I'm the salesman. I left a message."

"You're the one selling questions. My dad said your business plan didn't make sense."

"High praise from a funeral director slash hotelier," said the man.

"Why are you following me?"

"I told you on the phone. I'm selling questions."

"What questions?"

"I mostly specialize in IAQs. That's Infrequently Asked Questions."

"Such as what?"

"The answer to that question would inevitably be an answer and I am not in the business of selling answers. The exchange rate is terrible at the moment."

"How much do they cost, then, these questions of yours?"

"You're in luck. Today, and today only, I'm offering three questions for the price of one."

"But what is the price of one?"

"One of my questions is worth six of yours and since you have kindly donated those, I will now repay you with the three you are owed. My first question for you is this... Where are the bodies?"

"What bodies?" asked Campbell.

"If you'll excuse my use of the dreaded D-word, the dead bodies. The late Mayor Kendall, the sadly missed Doctor Good, the dearly departed Madam Letrec and Mr. Ravenscroft – rest his soul. Where are their bodies?"

"The bodies are kept in the mortuary until the funeral."

"I see."

"Mrs. Simm will be making them presentable for the big event," continued Campbell.

"Then perhaps we should move on to your second question." The salesman paused, as though trying to recall his next line. "What has your father got to hide?"

Hearing this question spoken out loud rather than at the back of his mind had a powerful effect on Campbell. He felt tears of relief spring to his eyes that the question should occur to someone else. His father, Mr. Milkwell, was an upstanding member of society. People respected him. He rubbed shoulders with the town's brightest and best. Campbell had never heard anyone ask the question that had plagued him his whole life. What did his father have to hide? Was it really a coincidence that all those competing hotels had suffered such terrible fates? Why was theirs the only funeral business in town? What secrets lurked in the slowly sinking walls of the funeral home?

In spite of his doubts, Campbell repeated the words he had heard his father saying so many times over the years. "My father has grafted all his life, through all the bad days and the good."

"Ah, the good old days. Back when The Roof ran this town. You've heard of him, of course? Back then people believed in him because he made them believe. They feared him because he put the fear into them. His empire was built on a hill of corpses, many of which were never found. Did you know that without a body it's very hard to bring a murder case? Something happened to them. Someone made them disappear. And who better to get rid of bodies than an undertaker?" He opened his briefcase and pulled out a dock leaf. "That was a rhetorical question, by the way. I throw them in free of charge. You don't mind if I . . . ?" He rolled up the dock leaf and sucked hard at one end, drawing out the moisture until it went limp and soft.

"What proof do have you of any of this?"

"I don't need proof." He crushed the soggy dock leaf in his fist and tossed it into a nearby bin. "The only conviction I am interested in is my conviction to ask questions. I have no proof that your father built a funeral business on a mountain of murdered men. Nor can I show photographs of the rival hotels being picked off one by one. Now, your final question: what is the link between the previous two questions?"

"The link between the location of the bodies and what my father has to hide?"

"Let us consider the four victims of this terrible accident. Mayor Kendall, who came to office during the reign of The Roof. She worked for him. She covered up his indiscretions. And yet when The Roof was betrayed, she did not fall. In fact, she prospered, which means..." He paused and looked at Campbell.

"That she was involved in the betrayal."

"Very good. Next, our poor demised doctor performed some of the most abhorrent crimes imaginable without ever facing the consequences, which leads us to the conclusion that..."

"Someone was protecting him." Campbell finished the salesman's sentence.

"We've all seen the documentary about Mr. Ravenscroft's attempts to create an army of dead bodies, and who doesn't know the story of Madam Letrec's elongated youthfulness."

"But all this was ages ago," said Campbell. "*The Roof* died before I was born."

"And if he didn't? If he was only now returning to power, then it would make sense that those who betrayed him would need to finally face justice."

"But how could he return? Why? When? Where?"

The salesman chuckled. "Why? When? Where? Yes, this is the thing about dealing in questions," he said. "They're so very moreish, don't you find?"

3.

Campbell found his father in the back room, ironing neat folds into the hearse curtains.

"You're late," said Mr. Milkwell. "This is not the week for dawdling."

"I didn't dawdle." Campbell was still feeling shaken by the conversation with the salesman. He had spent his entire life avoiding the questions he had about his father. But now those questions had been voiced and it was impossible to ignore them. "Most people feel sad at funerals. I was wondering if you felt sad," he said.

"Emotions are unprofessional," replied Mr. Milkwell.

"So you do have them?"

"What's the matter with you?" snapped his father. "This is a big day for us. It's all of our Christmases at once, with a few Easters and a bank holiday Monday thrown in for good luck."

"Four people died," said Campbell. "Four people got torn to death in the center of town by a wild animal that no one has even seen."

"One's passing can come in many forms. Some fall asleep and never awake, others suffer pain or discomfort. Some are torn to death in the middle of a waxwork museum by an escaped animal. The end result is the same."

The reception bell rang.

"Sorry. We're not taking bookings this week," shouted Mr. Milkwell.

"Oh, I don't want to stay." The salesman appeared at the doorway.

"This is the man who left the message," said Campbell. "He sells questions."

"Actually, I've moved on from questions," said the salesman. "People simply aren't inquisitive enough these days." He shook his head sadly. "I'm now in the business of selling after-life insurance."

"What's that mean?" asked Campbell.

"Life insurance," said his father. "It's when you make regular payments to a company so that when you die, your family are looked after financially." He turned to address the salesman. "We're fully covered, thank you."

"I didn't say life insurance. I said after-life insurance," said the salesman. "One down payment for a guaranteed place in the after-life."

Mr. Milkwell smiled, but Campbell could tell his father's patience was wearing thin. "We're covered for that too, thank you." The phone began to ring. "I'd better get that."

"The problem with after-life insurance is that no one knows for sure what happens after death," said the salesman. "You can put all your faith in one insurer only to discover upon death that you threw your lot in with the wrong one."

"I'm not worried about that," said Mr. Milkwell, glancing at the ringing phone.

"You are really that certain that you have the right insurer?"

"I'm happy with my current policy, yes."

"You must have a good insurance company. Perhaps you can furnish me with their details."

"Sorry. No. Campbell, get the phone. It may be important"

Campbell answered the phone. "Hello? Milkwell's Funeral and Guest House."

"I can only help you if you help me," said the salesman.

"What help do I need?" asked Mr. Milkwell.

"You need to locate the bodies."

"The bodies?"

"Dad," said Campbell. "It's Mrs. Simm on the phone."

"I should take this," said Mr. Milkwell. "This is our make-up artist. She's preparing the guests for today's event."

"She says the bodies are missing," said Campbell.

"Missing?" exclaimed Mr. Milkwell.

"She popped out to buy Madam Letrec's eye-liner. When she returned, they were gone."

"Gone? Where?"

"The address of your insurer, please," said the salesman. "Where is he? My employer has a proposition for him but his number is ex-directory."

Mr. Milkwell looked at the salesman as though he had, only now, recognized him. "Your employer," he said.

"The address, please."

"You'll return the bodies if I tell you?" said Mr. Milkwell.

"I'll have them returned at once."

Mr. Milkwell scribbled something down on the telephone notepad and handed it to the salesman.

He looked at it and smiled. "Thank you. The bodies will be back with your make-up artist within the hour."

"Once you have delivered the message to your boss, I would be grateful to talk over another matter with you," said Mr. Milkwell. "After all, two businessmen such as we are should not allow our employers' disputes to get in the way of opportunities."

"What opportunity?" asked the salesman.

"Perhaps I can help answer some of your own questions."

"What questions?"

"I believe the common one when it comes to one's own past: why me? Why these things happened to me."

The salesman touched the back of his neck as though experiencing a twinge of pain. "I'll put some thought into it." The salesman turned and walked out. Campbell put the phone down and said, "What? *He* took the bodies?"

"It's nothing," said his father. He wrote something down on another piece of notepaper. Campbell couldn't see what he wrote and Mr. Milkwell was quick to fold the paper and seal it in an envelope.

"I don't understand. Why did he waste my time asking all those questions?"

"He was never selling questions. A salesman like that only deals in mischief," said Mr. Milkwell. "Now, focus. Take this to the ice cream parlor immediately."

"Mr. Morricone's?"

"Yes. It's a note about the order for the buffet at the wake."

"There's going to be ice cream at the wake?"

"Of course. Ice cream is the perfect dish for wakes. It is cold, comforting and it makes one feel as though one were starting afresh."

4·

Mr. Morricone read the note and screwed up the piece of paper. "How about a Dark Berry Betrayal for the road?" he said.

"Sorry, I haven't any money," said Campbell.

"This one is on the house."

No one ever refused a free ice cream from Mr. Morricone so Campbell accepted and sat down in a booth to eat it. Mr. Morricone squeezed his large frame into the seat opposite him.

"You've known my father a long time," said Campbell, tasting the crimson sauce drizzled over the milk-white ice cream.

"We go back a long way," said Mr. Morricone. "We were friends in the good old days, you know."

"Do you know if he has anything to hide? From back then, I mean."

Mr. Morricone pulled a handkerchief from his top pocket and wiped a dab of chocolate sauce off the menu. "All parents must have their mysterious ways."

"Why?"

"To hide their imperfections. We were children before we were parents and all children make mistakes. We all did things we were ashamed of. Had we known back then that we would have children to answer to, maybe we would have acted differently. But, you see, before you were born you meant nothing to us and no child likes to be reminded of that."

Campbell half understood this. "So do you have children, then, Mr. Morricone?"

"Oh yes. Lots. Not all close, but all important to me."

"I'm worried that my father's secret is that he killed someone."

Mr. Morricone sighed. "You have to remember that back when *The Roof* still reigned, back in the good old days, people didn't fear death in the same way. They knew they would be looked after. These days, everyone is so greedy, so impatient."

"You didn't answer my question."

Mr. Morricone picked up Campbell's empty bowl and stood up. "I'm afraid I sell ice cream, not answers."

On Campbell's walk home, there were constant reminders about the big event. Every newspaper headline, every billboard or bus advert had something to say about it. All of the shops in the center of town were cashing in on it. Hairdressers offered funeral cuts for the men and mourning perms for the ladies. Shoe shops displayed the perfect footwear for the funeral. Flower shops competed for the most sombre wreaths. Pubs had boards outside with the names of specially brewed beers such as Letrec's Last Breath, Ravenscroft's Crafty Ale, Kendall's Keg and Dr Good's Medical Miracle. Even the graffiti artists had created murals of the dead. On the side of *The Big Heart* someone had scrawled the words, *LARKIN MILLS NEEDS A NEW ROOF.*

Back at the funeral parlor, there were four horse-drawn carriages waiting outside and four of the most spectacular coffins Campbell had ever seen in the reception. His father was buzzing around them like a bottle moth with a duster. He wore white gloves and was busily ensuring that the brass was gleaming.

"Ah, Campbell. Message delivered?" he said.

"Yes," responded Campbell.

"Then it is out of our hands."

"The ice cream order?"

"Yes, precisely that. Come and have a look at what a good job Mrs. Simm has done with Madam Letrec. Apparently every nail had to be glued back onto her hand. Old skin is so much less forgiving than young. Mrs. Simm says she hardly used any blusher as Madam Letrec's complexion in death was not hugely different to the one she had in life. Thankfully, most of the scarring was not on the face, unlike poor Mr. Ravenscroft."

"Scars from an animal no one has caught."

"Not this again."

"Yes, this again. Why was there no investigation into their deaths?"

"What is there to investigate? Everyone knows what happened. It's hardly a mystery"

"It's not exactly a normal way to die, is it?"

"I didn't say it was common. I said there was nothing worthy of an investigation. There was nothing suspicious."

"What about all of the other people you've disposed of over the years? Were none of those deaths suspicious?"

His father's expression darkened. "Disposed of? I don't think I like that phrase."

"Why? It's just another way to say dead. Dispensed with, terminated, murdered. These are all ways of avoiding the D-word."

Mr. Milkwell removed his white gloves carefully, one finger at a time. "These questions," he said. "You got them from that salesman, did you? Of course you did. It's easy to sell questions to the young. Their curiosity is indiscriminating."

"What's wrong with being curious?"

"It's too often misdirected. The answers you seek are right here." He tapped his own chest. "But you won't listen to me, will you? Then some salesman appears out of nowhere with a briefcase full of dock leaves and a fancy watch, and you buy every question he has to sell."

"Where is he? Did he come back? Was it him that took the bodies? Why? What did he want?"

"Enough questions. He won't be troubling us again. He's sold his last question. He's knocked on his last door in Larkin Mills."

"Why? Where's he gone?"

"He is no longer a concern. He has moved on. He has departed."

"He's dead?'

"Campbell, you've been acting very disrespectfully recently but this adolescent rebellion ends here. You understand me?

One day you will inherit this business but you must learn to trust me first. You do want to be an undertaker one day, don't you?"

"I . . . " Campbell had never questioned that he would one day inherit the family business. What else would he do? He had occasionally questioned some of the murkier corners of his father's past but he had always respected him for all he had achieved. Through the good times and the bad, his father had toiled. Campbell would do the same. He would do him proud.

"So do we have a problem here or can we get on with the job in hand?" asked Mr. Milkwell.

"No problem," said Campbell. "Let's get on."

5.

Everyone agreed that the funeral was one of the best days in the history of the town. Those old enough said it reminded them of the good old days because everyone pulled together and felt connected. As predicted, the television ratings were unprecedented for such an event. Not everything went according to plan but the inevitable mishaps were soon forgotten, such as the fatality on the ring road during the procession. One of the television commentators spoke at length about what a great honor it would be to die on such a prestigious day.

After a speech by Mayor Kendall's son, Ivor, and a specially commissioned concerto by the Larkin Mills Busking Orchestra, there was another procession to the crematorium and a fireworks display before the cremation.

As the four coffins were lifted onto the conveyor belt, Campbell couldn't help but notice that the men carrying Madam Letrec's coffin were straining more than you would expect considering she was the lightest of the lot. It was almost as though her coffin contained a second body. Campbell breathed in the rich aroma of the burning coffin. It smelled like human flesh and dock leaves. He looked at his father, standing with his head bowed, respectfully, solemnly, savoring every moment. Campbell felt a pang of pride. Why shouldn't his father enjoy himself? He had worked all his life for this moment. This was his Queen Victoria. It was a day that Campbell would remember for the rest of his life. Why would he want to ruin that with questions? Why would he rock the boat? Why would he challenge his father?

He would not.

The Consolation of Ice Cream

1.

I WAS WALKING BACK from my father's funeral when I saw
the queue for Mr. Morricone's Ice Cream Parlor. Ross was
waiting for me back at the orphanage but it was an unsea-
sonably hot day and my throat was dry. In his final days, my
father talked a lot about his terrible, unquenchable thirst, but
that wasn't the reason he told me to remove the egg from his
presence. He told me he had achieved everything he set out to
achieve. He told me he was finally at peace.

I took my place at the back of the long queue, hoping the
ice cream might take away my thirst and, with it, my sadness.
Stupid, I know. It was only ice cream. While I waited, I listened in on a couple of tourists talking about what they were
going to do next.

"I hear Madam Letrec's World of Wax is open again," said

the man.

"So soon after all those people died there?" said his wife.

"That's why it's opened. They've recreated the room where it happened with all four people being torn apart, made entirely from wax."

"Bit gory, isn't it?"

"The queue for that is even longer than this," said the husband. "So what are you going to get when you get to the front?"

"Either a Raspberry Rapture Ripple or a Fudge Flood. What about you?"

"Apparently the Sacrificial Sorbet is to die for."

I noticed a man across the road. He wore a straw hat, and a red and white checkered overall. He had a tray in front of him, held in place by straps around his shoulders. No one had joined the queue behind me yet so I decided to cross the road to see what he was selling. His hat cast a dark shadow over his face but, as he looked at me, he smiled and I saw a set of dazzling white teeth.

"Good afternoon. Would you care for a refreshing cold tonic, Miss?" he said, showing me the tray. There were rows of brightly colored bottles with corks in the tops.

"What flavors do you have?" I asked.

"Only one. That which you most desire."

"I want something to quench my thirst."

"Yes, but what is it you're thirsting for?"

There was something familiar about his voice but I had never seen his face before.

"I was hoping for an ice cream but it's a very long queue."

When the man looked across the road I got the distinct impression that he was pretending to see the queue, even though there must have been at least a hundred people standing there.

"It can be frustrating waiting in line with everyone else, can't it?" he said. "You want what you want now, don't you?"

"I suppose." There was something off about his manner.

"You feel resentful of them, don't you? I understand. It's perfectly natural. All these people, standing in front of you. Why should they be rewarded before you, just because they arrived earlier? What if they eat up all the good stuff and leave you with the dregs? What if, after all that time, you get to the front only to find that there is nothing left for you?"

He spoke so softly, almost as though he was speaking inside my head.

"But that's how queues work," I said, doubting myself.

"Says who? Says him? The ice-cream dealer? Why is he in charge of how people should wait? Who made him the boss? You want your thirst quenched and you want it quenched now." He picked up a bottle and pulled out the cork. Light green vapor escaped from the top. He poured a splash into a cup. He picked up another bottle and repeated the action. This one was red and it hissed as he opened it. He continued adding and mixing seven in total. He placed another cup upside down on the first then shook them vigorously.

When he handed it to me, I could see that the liquid inside was oily black with a thick, syrupy consistency. It looked revolting. "What is it?" I asked.

"It is that which you most desire. Try it."

It may have been his persuasive words or the darkness of my mood after the funeral but I didn't even pause to consider. I gulped it down in one. I am unable to describe the taste. I do not have the words, except that it was the taste of everything I had ever wanted from life. My head swam. When I finished it,

I went into instant mourning for that feeling.

"How much do I owe you?" I asked.

The man smiled. "Owe me?"

"Money," I said, reaching into my pocket and pulling out a handful of coins. "I must pay you."

"I don't want your money," said the man. "I want your help. I have an excellent product, but no advertising. Mr. Morricone has all these tourists queuing up for his inferior product but no one is interested in mine."

"You want me to spread the word?"

"Yes, spread the good word. If you can get me a queue longer than his I will reward you with a free drink."

"Easy."

I went back across the road to begin work. I selected a large man with a sweaty back who kept shifting from foot to foot, while grumbling about how slowly the queue was moving.

"Excuse me, are you looking for something to quench your thirst?" I asked.

"No pushing in," said the woman behind him, who had a sleeping toddler in a pushchair.

"I'm not pushing in," I said.

"Don't try asking me to buy you one either," said the man. "You have to join the back of the queue."

"That's right," said the woman. "This queue is here for a reason."

"Yes, I know," I said, "but if you're looking for the most amazing taste sensation in the world you should go and see that man across the road." I pointed at the drinks vendor, standing on his own.

"I don't want a drink," said the man. "I want an ice cream."

I was getting frustrated. "How about I keep your place? You can buy a drink while you're waiting."

"No holding places," said the woman.

"I saw someone hold your place just a minute a go," said the man. "You went to the toilet."

"I have a weak bladder," she said.

"How about you both go?" I said. "I'll save both your places."

"Fine with me," said the businessman standing behind the woman.

The conversation had drawn the attention of lots of people with nothing else to do, so they watched as the man and woman approached the drinks vendor. He mixed their drinks then handed them the cups. Everyone saw the expression of pure ecstasy on the man's face as he drank. The woman drank next. The toddler woke up and started crying but she didn't notice. I think if you had asked her while she was drinking, she would not even have remembered she had a child. Neither of them returned to the queue. Both walked away happy.

I didn't have to do much after that. More followed, intrigued to experience what they had just witnessed. The drinks vendor didn't speed up the process so a new queue soon formed. I carried on working along Mr. Morricone's line but it was easy now people could see others were leaving in their droves. In under an hour, the drinks vendor had a longer queue than Mr. Morricone. I crossed the road and went to the front.

"No pushing in," said a plain-looking man holding a briefcase.

"I'm not pushing in," I said. "I work for him."

"Do you?" said the drinks vendor.

"I did what you asked," I said. "I got you a longer queue."

"In which case you can consider your debt paid."

"But you said I could get another drink," I said.

"Of course," he replied. "That's fine. You'll have to join the queue, of course, but once you get to the front you will have your free drink."

I looked with dismay at the long line of people. "But, you said—"

"I said you could get a free drink. I said nothing of queue jumping." He finished mixing the drink and handed it to the man with the briefcase. "Here," he said. "I'm sorry to hear about your mother. Garden party season will never be the same without her lemonade." The vendor turned back to me. "The end of the queue," he said.

"Excuse me, it's me next," said a woman in a trouser suit.

"Then me," said the man behind her.

While the queue for the drinks vendor snaked back down the road, Mr. Morricone's line was down to the final ten people. I considered joining it but I no longer wanted an ice cream. The very thought of it made me shiver.

2.

It was by far the hottest day of the year so Mr. Morricone was surprised to serve his final customer.

"It's him across the road," said an elderly lady. "He's stealing your customers. It shouldn't be allowed."

Mr. Morricone made her Aniseed Apocalypse, then stepped out from behind the counter and looked out of the window. He recognized him at once, in spite of the fact that he looked different each time he had seen him. Finchley, Miguel, Larkin, his look changed as often as his name but his nature was consistent. He was goading him, hoping to get a reaction. Usually, Mr. Morricone would have ignored him but performing such a low trick on such a perfect day for ice cream was unacceptable.

He stepped outside, pulled down the shutters in front of the shop and crossed the road.

"All out. Sorry, folks. See you tomorrow," said the drinks vendor, seeing him approach.

The crowd sighed. Some shouted insults. Some looked to Mr. Morricone in hope but most were too embarrassed, knowing that by crossing that road, they had betrayed him. One by one, the disappointed crowd dispersed, leaving the two men alone in the street.

"So," said Mr. Morricone. "Your salesman found me and now you've got my attention. What do you want?"

"To talk about the good old days. I know you remember them. Your customers tell me you're always harping on about them. We worked so well together back then."

Mr. Morricone grinned. "I miss the order. Everything was so much more controlled back then. So much neater."

"That's the thing about tyranny. It is rather neat."

"Whereas you would allow the world to descend into the chaos of selfishness."

"One can only descend if one knows which way is up," replied the drinks vendor.

"You always did have a fondness for riddles."

"You and me both."

"These days I prefer stories."

"Is there a difference?"

"Of course. A riddle is a problem to be solved. A story is a solution to be questioned."

The drinks vendor laughed. "Only you could argue against riddles with a riddle. This is precisely why they flocked to me, you know. You're too obscure. You're too mysterious."

Mr. Morricone turned to leave. "The loyal ones will return.

I only care about them."

"Ice cream," said Finchley, shaking his head. "That's what you have been reduced to. A sweet dessert that melts as fast as you can eat it."

"Ice cream makes people happy," snapped Mr. Morricone. "And yet I stole your entire queue with the promise of something new, something immediate."

"Your tonics will never be as satisfying as my product."

"I'll admit that there was something good about the feeling of being under your wing. I never felt so safe as when I worked for you back then."

"So why did you betray me?"

"I suppose I didn't want to worship you any longer."

"Do you want to know why I kept this business a secret from you? Because I realized the only way to win was to stop competing. I realized that you enjoy the competition too much."

"So you hid away in this quiet road with your ice cream and your sprinkles and your special sauces, leaving everyone else to suffer with me."

"Yes," said Mr. Morricone. "While you tried and failed to control this town, I focused on something people actually want."

"Ice cream?" scoffed the drinks vendor.

Mr. Morricone sighed. "What do you want?"

"I've changed."

"People like us, we don't change."

"That's not true. Back in the good old days you were all about the righteous vengeance. You were fun back then."

"Get to the point."

"You were right about this place. It's grown on me. I think we could make it better if we worked together again."

"I don't operate like that any more. What your demon did to those poor people in the waxwork museum was horrific."

"A sacrifice for you. I delivered your betrayers to you."

"I never asked for that."

"If you're so blameless then what happened to my salesman?"

"I cannot be held responsible for what others do in my name. Mr. Milkwell's intentions were honorable."

"Don't you understand anything, old man? I am trying to apologize."

Mr. Morricone's laughter was low but genuine. "Is that what this is? An apology?"

"Reconciliation. That's what I want."

"We've tried this before. As soon as I turn my back you'll be plotting something."

"Not this time. I want to come and work for you."

"In the ice cream parlor?"

"If that is what you wish. We used to work so well together, you and I. I would be happy mopping the floors if I was forgiven. That is what I most desire." He got down on one knee. The bottles fell from his tray and smashed on the pavement. Their colorful contents spilled into the drains. He made no effort to pick them up.

Mr. Morricone lifted his chin, then took his hand and helped him to his feet.

"I forgive you," he said. "We'll be equal partners this time."

A smile spread across the drinks vendor's face. "You see?" he said. "You are capable of change after all. Partners."

3.

The day after her father's funeral, Park told me she had something to return to the ice cream parlor. I tagged along because she let me. Now she had moved into the orphanage, Park and I were pretty much inseparable, which was how I liked it.

"What's in there?" I asked.

"You worried it's a human head, Ross?" She waved the bag in my face.

"No," I said, although the thought had occurred to me.

"This is what I'm returning."

When we reached the shop, I noticed that the old sign had been taken down but a new one had not yet been put up. A sign on the door read, *CLOSED FOR REFURBISHMENT.* I was happy to turn away and come back another day, but Park tried the door and forced it open. Mr. Morricone and another man were busily working behind the counter. Wearing identical checkered hats and white overalls, the two men looked strikingly similar to each other.

"Sorry. We're closed," said Mr. Morricone.

"We'll be open again next week," said the other man.

"So you're working together now?" said Park.

"That's right. I'm changing the name. No longer is this Mr. Morricone's Ice Cream Parlor. It is now Mr. Morricone and Mr. Morricone's Ice Cream Parlor. Isn't that right, Mr. Morricone?" He licked chocolate sauce off a spoon.

"Mr. Morricone and I are putting the past behind us."

"You are them," said Park. "You are the two aliens my father told me about."

"Aliens?" I repeated.

She wasn't looking at me. "You are the dwarf and the sooth-sayer. You are The Roof and Finchley. You are God and the devil."

"These days we prefer Mr. Morricone and Mr. Morricone," said Mr. Morricone.

I laughed because I was unsure what else I could do.

"You assume different forms and you are always fighting each other and turning everyone else into players in your stupid game," said Park.

"That does sound like us," said Mr. Morricone.

"Doesn't it just?" agreed Mr. Morricone.

"I have something that belongs to you." Park opened the bag she was holding. One of the Mr. Morricones pulled out a large grey egg.

"The Egg of Life," said Mr. Morricone.

"I don't know why you call it that when it brings death."

The other Mr. Morricone took a bottle of syrup and poured it into a bowl of yellow goo. He stirred it in with a large wooden spoon. "Death gives meaning to life."

"That's what my father thought," said Park.

"Did it make your father as happy as he had hoped it would?" asked one Mr. Morricone.

"It killed him," said Park.

"Yes, but did it make him happy?" asked the other.

"Yes," she admitted.

I was feeling confused and it wasn't just the conversation. The air inside the parlor was thick with rich aromas. There were bowls of gloopy chocolate sauce all along the counters. Mr. Morricone dipped a biscuit cone into a bubbling pan of sauce and placed it on a tray so that the brown sauce ran down the side like lava from a volcano.

The other Mr. Morricone held up the egg and squeezed. A droplet of purple liquid splashed into a bowl of molten caramel.

"You are wicked," said Mr. Morricone.

"It'll be like the old days," said the other. "A little bit of life, a little bit of death."

"I don't get it," I said. "Which one is which?"

The two men stared back at me in innocent confusion.

"I mean, which of you is God and which is the devil?" I said. "Who's good and who's evil? You seem as bad as each other."

"Yes," said Park. "And why would God work with the devil, anyway?"

Mr. Morricone lifted up a jar of rainbow sprinkles and tipped it onto the counter so that it created a small, colorful mound that changed color as the tiny specks rolled down the side. "Do you know the thing about ice cream?" he said. "It's not just that it makes people happy. It's not just the infinite possibilities it opens up. The thing about it is that you can't eat too much. If you do you'll be sick. If you eat it too quickly, you'll get a headache. Ice cream, like everything else, must be taken in moderation."

"What does that mean?" I asked.

"I think what my friend is trying to say is that both of us are formed of good and bad. We've each done things we are proud of and things we are ashamed of. Like everyone else, we're looking for the perfect balance."

I felt unsteady on my feet. The smells were awakening my taste buds. They were confusing my other senses. I began to wonder if there really were two Mr. Morricones.

"Come and work with us. We'll need plenty of help when we start up the business again."

Each Mr. Morricone held out a small tub of ice cream. One was chocolate-brown with thin squiggles of white sauce over its surface. The other was deep purple dotted with generous chunks of fruit. They both looked irresistible. I leaned in but Park took my hand and stopped me dead.

"We don't want to work for you," she said. "You can keep your egg and your ice cream; we're going to go into business for ourselves."

"Doing what?" asked Mr. Morricone.

"We're going to make our own ice cream. We're going to find a better spot and we're going to take your customers."

"You think you can take us on?" said Mr. Morricone.

"We're going to try."

"People have tried and failed before." Mr. Morricone took a knife and crushed a chunk of crystallized ginger. "What makes you any different?"

"Because we don't believe in you," said Park. "We believe in each other."

She tugged my hand and dragged me out of the gloomy shop into the brilliant sunshine. As soon as we stepped out I felt clear-headed again. A bus was approaching so we ran to the stop and jumped on. We didn't return to the ice cream parlor after that.

Park and I had our own plans.

Decision to Burn

ENCASED IN AN ICE PRISON floating in a vacuum of noth-
ingness, I finally understood that my attempt to overthrow my father had always been doomed to failure from the
beginning. He truly was all powerful. I looked at the sorrowful
sight of my demon snoring in the corner of the room, curled up
with its horned head, resting on its hooved hands. It was such
a revolting sight I turned back to my own reflection in the ice
in search of beauty, but my face was no longer the picture of
perfection. There were two small protrusions at my temples
where my skin had been smooth before.

"They're a reminder," said my father's voice.

"So it is true, then. You really are everywhere."

"I'm everywhere I want to be, yes." My father's face appeared
in one of the walls.

"So you saw everything?" I said.

"Yes, I saw it all; your growing dissatisfaction, your attempts
to gain supporters, your creation of this thing." He looked

down at my demon.

"You could have stopped me earlier," I said sullenly.

He nodded.

"What did you get out of watching my pathetic attempts to take your place?"

My father's smile didn't suit him. "I wouldn't call them pathetic. You made some good speeches, you had a perfectly valid plan, and you actually succeeded in creating life . . . sort of."

"But you could have crushed me at any point."

"Certainly. I am everywhere. I see everything, I created this universe. Do you have any idea what that feels like?"

I rolled my eyes. "Obviously not."

"It's so dull," said my father.

"Dull?"

"Utterly tedious. I enjoyed your little rebellion. For a bit back there it felt as though I wasn't in control, even though I was, of course. I even took on various roles to help you. You do know I can change form, don't you?"

"I do now."

"I was your lieutenant. I was your sergeant. That angel who found you the materials to make this . . . What do you call it?"

"A demon."

"Yes, your demon. Good name, by the way. I lived through you. I understood your struggle. There were moments when I genuinely felt as though I was on your side."

"You were on my side in my struggle to depose you?" My laughter bounced off the icy walls. It sounded hollow and cold.

"This bitter war you have been waging against me has been the most excellent diversion. In a universe that holds so few surprises for me, you provided some welcome escapism. For that, I thank you."

"This is your way of thanking me?" I said. "Encasing me in ice for all eternity?"

"What are you talking about? I've provided an escape route."

An unlit wood fire appeared in the center of the prison and I saw that we were no longer suspended in space; on the other side of the ice walls was a wooded hill. The distant stars were above us and obscured by the swaying trees. Beneath my feet strange vegetation squeezed its way through the icy floor.

"Light the fire, melt the ice and you can walk free."

"Where are we?" I asked.

"It's a place called Earth."

I pulled up a plant by its roots. They were covered in grainy, crumbly dirt. "Yes, I can see why," I said. "There's something different about this place. What's that smell?"

"It's the stench of mortality." My father stepped through a wall as though it was nothing. He was showing off, as usual. He picked up a large oval object from behind one of the trees and returned to the prison.

"What does that mean? What is that?" I peered at the object. "It's an egg, of course, but it is an egg with a difference. Whereas most eggs provide life, this one provides death."

"Death?" It was the first time I had heard the word.

"It's new. Try it." He handed me the egg. "I think you'll like it. A little squeeze should be enough."

I held the egg over a small fern growing by my feet. I squeezed the egg and a droplet of purple liquid appeared at the base. It fell onto the plant, which instantly withered and crumbled. It was the most beautiful sight I had ever seen. "I like it," I said.

"I knew you would. The egg contains the essence of death.

Applied in pure form, as you can see, it brings instantaneous disintegration, but when it is woven in at the moment of creation, it means that life here develops small faults over time. Nothing on this planet lasts forever. Not one thing."

"I don't understand."

"Of course you don't. You are immortal, like myself. Consider yourself lucky that I made you before I came up with this idea."

"So you would abandon me, an immortal, on a planet that will not last?"

"I didn't say it wouldn't last," said my father. "Life here must replicate itself to survive. Individuals do not last but the animals and vegetation have the ability to reproduce. I think you'll find much to marvel at on this planet. It is my greatest achievement. That's why I am stopping. I am done with creation."

"You're stopping because you've finally made something that isn't perfect?" I scoffed. "You've made life that will always fail and decay?"

"Death isn't a failure. The fleeting quality of existence here makes it all so much more beautiful." He picked up a handful of dust and threw it straight through the ice ceiling into the night sky, making the buzzing moths in the branches glow brightly.

"Will I be subject to this death too if I stay here? Will I die?"

"The bodies you adopt will wear out but you will remain immortal."

"I must take another form to live here?"

"Yes. There are plenty of life forms to choose from: slithering ones, swimming ones, crawling ones and flying ones. My personal favorite is a relatively new addition, a species I made in my own image. I call them humans."

A strangely hairy two-legged ape-like creature in ragged clothing stepped into the clearing. He looked at us in awe. He placed a hand on the ice wall. As he felt its coldness, he cried out in pain and withdrew it. My father raised his hands and a dazzling light appeared around him. The creature dropped to the ground and bowed in fear.

"So you've bred a species of simple-minded servants designed to worship you," I said.

"Not in the least," said my father. "These humans have come a long way. Down from the trees, at least. They're doing remarkably well for creatures with such short life-spans."

"So what is to stop me making myself into a great and powerful leader of these humans?"

"Absolutely nothing. Give it a try. I give you a couple of life-times before you grow tired of the adulation."

"Have you grown tired of it, then?" I asked bitterly.

"That's what I've been trying to explain. Absolute power is absolutely boring."

"So why did you crush my rebellion?"

"Oh, you wouldn't have enjoyed winning if you had known I had let you win."

I pressed my head against the ice wall and examined the bowing creature. There was something crawling through its matted hair. Even with the ice between us, I could tell it stank even worse than the rest of the place. I banged my fist on the wall and the creature fled into the wood. I laughed to see something so full of fear and ignorance.

"This is a fresh opportunity," said my father.

"To do what?"

"To challenge me. To organize this world as you think it

should be organized."

"What if I don't want order? What if I want chaos?"

"You can do whatever you want. I give you free reign."

"You'd have me try again so you can stop me? Is that it? I am like a toy for you to play with."

"Not at all. I don't even have total control here."

"How is that possible?"

"Because I gave these humans the ability to think for themselves. They can decide to walk in the light or the darkness. It's up to them."

"So the choice you're offering me is to sit here in ice or light the fire and live," I said. "How is this even a choice?"

"The decision to burn should not be taken lightly," said my father.

"I wondered how long it would be before you delivered one of your obscure statements."

"It's tiresome, knowing what people are going to say, isn't it?" said my father. "Imagine how I feel."

"Will you be down here on this planet too?"

"Sometimes I pop down, you know, to give them a push in the right direction. An invention, a question, a notion... a hint. They often get the wrong end of the stick, of course. When I first showed them a harp, they used it as a weapon. One of them killed six of his own tribe before I took it off him. It was too soon."

"What will happen to my demon?"

"He's your responsibility now. You made him just as I made you. He is your child as you are mine. I think you will be surprised by how much time you spend worrying about him."

I looked at the malformed creature I had created, still snorting and snoring and snuffling in his sleep.

"He's not what I intended."

"So speaks so many parents," said my father. "Of course, if you don't want that responsibility, you can end it now."

He took the egg from my hands and squeezed. I cupped my hands and caught the droplet of thick purple liquid.

"Give your demon just one sip and you will not have to worry about him. He trusts you. He will drink it if you tell him to"

"Why does everything you do feel like a test?" I asked.

"Because you confuse tests with choices."

I looked at the demon. I had hoped to make a creature capable of war and destruction but ended up with this sorry excuse for a monster. This demon was the embodiment of my own failure. I brought my hands close to its open mouth. I smelled its rancid breath. I wouldn't even need to wake it. I could pour it straight in and watch him die.

"Harder than you'd think, isn't it?" said my father.

I stood up and opened my fingers. The poison hissed as it hit the icy floor. "I cannot end the thing I created," I admitted.

"I know how you feel," said my father. "No matter how much pain and trouble they give you, in the end they're your responsibility."

"Is that what I am? Your responsibility?" I snapped.

"I like to think of you more as a project."

"Why this spot? I know you wouldn't bring me to this spot without good reason."

He smiled. "You are right. It was here that I first came up with the idea of death. It was here that I created the egg. Death will always be more prominent in this place than elsewhere because this is death's birthplace."

"What's it called?"

"I was hoping you might help come up with a name."

My father vanished and I lit the fire. There was never any question I would. In my mind, it was no choice at all. The heat melted the ice but the flames burned my skin. My demon awoke, confused and frightened. He ran into the trees, clutching the egg. When the last embers of the great fire had died away, I stood in the clearing, and gazed up at the distant stars, wondering what to do next.

"It is very cold to be without one's robes," said a voice.

I turned to see a human, dressed in white and holding a lantern.

"That's funny," I replied. "It feels devilishly warm down here to me."